THE HIGHLAND KNIGHT'S REVENGE

LORI ANN BAILEY

Edited by Jess Snyder Edits and Quillfire Author Services

Cover Design by Dar Albert @ Wicked Smart Designs.

CHAPTER 1

*R*ose Citadel
   Gracious Hill, England, June 1193

R   *evenge.*
     That was the answer, but he couldn't
     remember the question or who had asked it.

Giric de Beaumont MacDonald squinted to get a better look at the man who sat two tables down. He'd just been informed the dark-haired man was Edward Linton, the son of Baron Gillingham, the Englishman who had come to Scotland and taken everything from him.

His enemy's son laughed with a petite brunette whose face was obscured by the man sitting on her other side. He wondered if Edward was aware the devil himself had fathered him. According to what he'd been told, Edwards's dark appearance and large build were the same as his sire. But Giric had never actually seen the English baron who killed his father.

Knowing he was so close to the man's family forced images of that dreadful day to the forefront of his mind, making them more real than the typical hazy scenes plaguing his waking hours and haunting his sleep. The only difference was that Edward wore a carefree smile instead of the scowl he'd envisioned on the man who cursed his dreams.

The bastard's son comported himself as if he were still a boy of fifteen and just learning the appeal of a lass. It was plain for all present that he was smitten with the lady at his side. Giric wished he could get a better look at her to see Edward's weakness.

He had waited eleven long years for the opportunity to meet his enemy. The Baron de Rose, Lord Yves, had given him this chance by inviting all the English nobles and knights to his castle for a tournament.

The coward who had killed Giric's father hadn't had the courage to make an appearance at the castle, sending his heir instead.

"Sir Giric?"

Squeezing his eyes shut to block out the rage that had pulled him back in time, back to plumes of smoke and the smell of burned wood and flesh, Giric turned toward the man at his side.

He took a deep breath. *Patience.* His vengeance would come soon now.

Meeting the other guest's questioning gaze, he plastered a smile upon his face. The man's eyes were framed by pale lids creased with age and too much awareness. His mealtime companion had once been a knight, but he'd been elevated to baron after the deaths of a nephew and his three older brothers. His father had been called Edward. It seemed the English had a fondness for the designation because Giric had been introduced to three other knights and an additional baron with the same name since his arrival.

"Pardon me. 'Twas a long journey, and I'll be a better companion after I've had a night's rest. What was yer question?" Giric gave his attention to the aging baron, who took a gulp from his wine goblet, then set it back down.

"What brings you here from Scotland?"

Revenge wasn't his only reason for making the journey south. "Lord Yves extended the invitation to my king, and William thought he should have some representation present." Giric didn't bother to mention he wasn't the only knight from Scotland in attendance.

"So, King William won't be joining us?" the baron asked.

Giric shook his head. "Nae. He had other matters requiring his attention."

"Pity, I would like to have met him. My lands are nearby on the border, and I think we would have some mutual interests."

"I'll see to it that he knows ye wish an audience. Mayhap when I am rested, we can converse again."

"I would enjoy that." The old man smiled.

"Please excuse me for now. I need to see that my squire and horse have been settled." He pushed back from the table and the generous feast their host had provided.

Giric had barely touched his food, but he needed air. The stuffy confines and loud sounds of a room filled with revelers gnawed at his nerves.

A plan was necessary. His king had sent him to find out where Lord Yves's loyalties lay, and he would find that answer, but his personal mission was in jeopardy. How was he to get his revenge without Baron Gillingham in residence?

Meandering out of the castle, he made his way toward the competition grounds, away from the throngs of people. As the clanging sounds of music and the noise of the crowds started to fade, he could think clearly again.

Throwing a gauntlet at the feet of his enemy upon his arrival had been Giric's original intention. He'd trained hard with King William's knights and was confident he could best most of the challengers in England.

But his prey wasn't here.

The son, Edward—he would be the answer. It might even be a fortuitous turn of fate to take the life of the man's son and let the arse live to endure a pain similar to what he'd experienced. But he wouldn't do that. He couldn't kill an innocent man. The son would not be recompense for his father's crime.

The scent of burning wood from campfires drifted toward him. Soft musical notes and distant revelry hummed a gentle murmur, blending with the sounds of nature. Glancing in that direction, his attention caught on a lone figure standing in the archery fields. It was a woman but from this distance and the fading light of day, he only knew her to be so by the dark blue gown and headpiece with gossamer fabric that billowed in the breeze. She gracefully pulled a quill from the pack sitting upright on the earth nearby.

Something about the scene was familiar. Like a child seeking reassurance after a nightmare and looking for comfort, he moved closer.

Leveling up with the shooting line, she squared her stance parallel with the target. Her spine was straight, and she rolled her shoulders back. She took aim, but instead of releasing the arrow, she paused. Her grip on the weapon loosened as she held her hand aloft. Shutting her eyes, the lass appeared to let the elements wash around her. Her graceful movements were like a dance with nature. The gentle breeze picked up, and gooseflesh rose on his arms.

Fear slapped him.

He was taken back to just before his father's death, reminded of the others who perished that day. A vision of the girl he couldn't save stabbed into his memory. She had been about twelve summers, and he'd been drawn to the scene then as well. Her brown hair had been cut at the shoulders, and the child had looked more like a pageboy than a young woman, but her nimble movements had captured him, much as the lass before him did now.

The lass from his memory and her father had been murdered the same day his father had…by Baron Gillingham.

He watched this lass let the arrow fly. He was so near that he could imagine a whizz as the shaft split the air and hit the target almost dead center, just as that child from the past had on the day he'd spied on her.

She pulled another arrow and repeated her ritual. She hit the mark, this time scoring better. He was amazed anyone could produce such results at that distance and with the dark of the evening starting to close in around them.

Motion caught his eyes as two men rushed toward her. Concern for her safety lashed at him. He hadn't been in time to save the child from his past, but he could make sure no harm befell this lass.

∼

J ennet Linton took aim and let the arrow loose. It landed slightly off the center. Not her best, but perhaps it was this headache and the strange environment she was now in. But she knew the truth— her world was shifting, and she'd finally be allowed the freedom she'd craved for years. And while that excited her, she also couldn't shake the feeling something would knock everything off course, just as fate did every time something good was supposed to happen.

With the promise of hope, there always came new misery.

Her father's health had deteriorated so much that he no longer recognized her or her two brothers. Although his mental decline had been progressing since her youth, his body and spirit had become frailer with each passing season. The healer who had attended to him for years said the baron would probably not survive through the harvest. In a way, it would be a relief to see him at peace.

Eddie had decided it was time to take charge and would be stepping into their father's place. No more keeping secrets. No more being tied to a life she hadn't chosen as they attempted to hide the severity of her father's fragility. But now, could she live up to her parents' wishes? They'd said she could marry for love, but did she have room in her heart for anyone outside the family?

She couldn't imagine trusting another with the truth of the past.

Glancing around, she saw people skirting the archery field, most already merry with spirits though the sun still gave enough light to illuminate her target. As a voice fell and rose, she spotted a bard spinning a tale in the encampment to the south. Jeers and laughs met his story, but she couldn't make out his words. Even if she'd wanted to, her mind couldn't focus beyond what her brother had shared with her this evening.

Assured no one would heed her movements—or at least confident those who would judge her were probably in the castle—she'd sneaked out to the place that always brought her clarity. Her head was pounding and she wasn't sure if it was because of the weight of her headpiece or the dawning revelation that although independence was what she'd wanted for years, something could go astray still. Her life might yet be tied to a circumstance she couldn't foresee.

Eddie had taken her arm as he escorted her down the hall and toward the feast. "I've asked Lord Robert if Ada and I might have permission to wed. He said yes."

She'd thrown her arms around him because it was the best possible news. Her best friend would be coming to live with them.

"I take it you are happy." He laughed.

"Of course I'd be pleased that Ada will be coming to our home."

That was when his look had turned, and he'd shifted his eyes away as though summoning his courage. "You will need to marry."

"But you, Father, and William need me." She'd been taking care of them for years—between her father's failing mental health, Edward's limp due to a fall from a horse several years ago, and William, her youngest brother, never knowing their mother.

"No. I'm grown now, and it's time I take responsibility. And you know Ada. She'll take good care of us."

Her chest had ached at his words, but they were the truth. He had become an admirable man. Once they made her father's condition known to the world, he'd have no problem taking over the duties of a baron. Edward had been taking on more the last few years, and she'd felt his resistance to her being at the helm of the household. And with Ada there, they wouldn't need her.

What would happen to her?

She'd grappled for a reason to stay. "But...I belong at Cresthaven." Images of a large stone estate, plush gardens, and sunny orchards that would soon be bursting with apples grazed her consciousness. It was their home in southern England, and although she'd desired a way out of being held back by duty, she'd never considered being forced to leave.

Edward had straightened to his full height and used a voice that she knew would identify him as a strong leader one day. He was ready for this, but she wasn't. "No. You don't. It is well past time you had your own family."

Her eyes had stung, and she couldn't explain her own reticence as they entered the great hall. She'd turned from him as pain ripped through her chest. "I know that."

"Then it's time you started acting like a sister instead of a mother. Pick a man from this tournament if you wish. I don't care who. After what we've been through, you deserve to be happy. But it's time. We all need to move on."

He was correct. At the age of twenty and three, it was long past when she should have wed and started her own family, but until recently, Edward had been too young and their father too frail.

After their conversation, she'd only nibbled at the bounteous feast laid out by their host, Lord Yves. As soon as she'd been able to, she'd made an excuse to retire early but instead had run to her chamber, grabbed her bow and quiver, and then set out for the fields.

She loosed her second arrow. It landed just beside the first, vibrating with the impact. Satisfied she was calm now and knowing that her brother had been correct, she started forward to collect her arrows before her return to the castle. She was startled when a dog ran in front of her, followed by two men who barreled after it, calling and promising the animal a morsel for its obedience.

"Pardon us," they blurted as they ran by.

A shiver ran down her spine, and she turned toward the castle only to notice a man had entered the field. He stood still, but it appeared as though he intended to rush toward her or the men. She followed his gaze as he analyzed the newcomers while they trotted off after the mutt.

Then his stare met hers and held.

Gooseflesh rose on the back of her neck and down her arms. The figure nodded some sort of acknowledgment, then he pivoted and marched back toward the castle. She let out a breath, and a strange awareness flowed through her, leaving her exposed in the large field with the cooling night air. The sensation left her thinking that her world had shifted twice in the same night.

CHAPTER 2

*G*iric's heart pounded a hectic warning as his fingers trembled. The vision of the woman in the field had shaken loose a brick in the foundation of his plans. His quest to avenge his father's death had been only a dream in the back of his head these last few years, but now that he had a chance at finding justice, it consumed him, and he was reading into things that weren't there.

That girl from the inn had perished with his father. He had seen her remains as remnants of the burned inn smoldered behind him. Perhaps smoke from the campfires had filtered into the part of his brain that couldn't let the past go. She was not here. This lass in the field couldn't be the girl from that fateful day.

Taking a deep breath, he turned toward the camp and vowed to focus on something else before anger consumed him. It was time to check on his squire, who had set a tent among the legion of others in attendance.

He wanted to make sense of what he'd glimpsed. Why had it affected him? Obviously, seeing his enemy's son had triggered an avalanche of despair and rage, along with images long buried. Feelings he'd managed to push away after his aunt, Ermengarde de Beaumont, the queen consort, had brought him into her home to live.

Since then, he'd become a trusted knight and guard of King William of Scotland. That confidence was what found him here in England now. Not to participate in the tournament, but to see what he could learn of their host.

The English evening fell sooner than that of a Scottish one in June. It had grown dark by the time he marched back into the great hall, intent on his royal mission. He was to determine if Lord Yves's loyalties lay with King Richard, who was off fighting for the crusades instead of leading his country, or John, who was rumored to be attempting a rebellion against his brother's administrators in the king's absence. His host's lands were at a strategic point in the north of England, and the baron's loyalties would disclose for King William what kind of neighbor he had.

The feast was nearing an end, and it appeared the tables were being pushed aside to make room for dancing. After circling the hall a few times with no sightings of his mysterious host, Giric determined the man had retired or was taking care of other business. Music began, and he turned to make his way up the stairs to his room. Exhaustion from the journey and the enormity of his tasks beat at him.

He froze as familiar blue skirts swished into his vision. He followed them upward to see a fair face with a headdress similar to the one from the form in the field. Her bow was gone, but he was fairly certain she was the archer. The woman swiveled to enter the space where the dancers gathered. He lost sight of her for a moment. Propelled by curiosity, he stepped onto the dance floor. A strange pull drew him toward her.

Guests circled for several moments before the music brought them together. He positioned himself so that she would be forced to partner with him. Their eyes met first, but she gave no sign of recognition, only a bonny smile in polite greeting. He had been a good distance away on the field.

When their hands touched, energy sizzled through him. Her eyes flared as if she'd been shocked by it too. He was mesmerized by her eyes, brown irises that surrounded large, dark pupils. No, that really didn't describe the color—the deep earthen shade was like a late night's embrace that promised sinful pleasures.

Her breath hitched as they slowly twirled, hands connected. Somehow, this common dance felt elicit and charged. Then they parted, but from the side of his vision, he saw her neck crane to follow his movements. Had she sensed something as well, or had he stared at her too intently?

Being in King William's court, he'd learned to dance well. His aunt had summoned him on many occasions to help her teach proper movements to some of the younger lasses at court. He could perform most of the courtly dances in his sleep, but no partner had ever caused his nerves to ignite in recognition.

The dance brought them back together. "Do ye always sneak off during a feast to practice with yer bow?"

Her eyes widened, and he knew he'd guessed correctly. It took her a moment, but when she recovered, she smiled. "Only when the guest list leads me to believe men who would spy on an innocent woman would be present."

He laughed, and they parted again.

When the music aligned them again, their hands met once more, and he noticed how dainty and soft hers were. "What if that knight was only trying to see to yer safety?" Not all men of his station were as chivalrous as they ought to be, but he hoped in offering her that bit of information, she'd give him some clue as to who she was.

"I think my skill speaks for itself. If you had come closer, you might have seen just how accurate I can be." Her eyes twinkled.

"Ye would no' welcome an emissary from King William more warmly?"

Before she could answer, a slender woman with long brown hair stumbled into them, then righted herself and apologized. Giric recognized the Scotsman who had flung the lass their way as a member of clan Ross. Nearby, one of the Sutherland twins seemed to resist the urge to reach out and pull the bonny lady into his arms.

Why would they be here? The rivals were most likely up to mischief, a distraction Giric could not afford. He steered his partner away from the feuding pair and the lass who had captured their attentions.

Then they separated again.

Moments later as they glided back toward one another, the scent of the summer breeze and fresh air came with her despite the close confines and crowd in the hall.

"I would not give my trust to anyone from Scotland before learning who they were."

What did she have against his home? He'd bet she'd never seen its beauty if she was so mistrustful of Scotsmen.

Her cheeks were red from exertion, or possibly it was this English heat. Even though they were near the border, the air here was not as temperate as that of the Highlands. And he now felt obliged to defend his homeland in her eyes.

"Then might I suggest a walk in the gardens? With yer aim, gaining yer confidence may be the only thing that saves my life."

She giggled, but then her brow furrowed just the slightest bit as she appeared to think over his proposal.

"I promise ye would be safe in my company and with so many about. I would no' do anything to dishonor you, my name, my king, or my country."

She remained silent. He thought she might refuse him. Perhaps she had a jealous suitor who would not take kindly to him wishing to spend time with her. Now that he'd seen her fair face, he wouldn't blame a man for holding tightly to such a lovely lass. He was presumptuous, but he had to know more about her. She was quiet for so long that he was about to make his excuses and turn to go when she nodded.

"I agree. But only for a short amount of time. You must rest for the jousting tomorrow. Have ye come to compete for the top honor?"

"Nae. But if 'twould win yer favor, I might change my mind."

Her cheeks reddened.

"You would be a lucky man. This is my first time attending a tourney, and I have never given anyone that honor."

The music paused, and they bowed.

The lass met his regard, and she began, "Shall I lead the way? I inspected the gardens upon my arrival."

"I have no' seen them yet, so I would be pleased to follow." An unfamiliar thrill blossomed in his chest as she led the way.

～

Jennet paused at a table to pick up a goblet of wine. The glass was almost as much to keep her hands busy as it was to quench her thirst. She found herself wanting to take the Highlander's strong palm and inspect the warm calluses she'd felt as they'd danced. He was a comely man with blond hair and eyes a shade darker than the blue of forget-me-nots that bloomed in the fields near her family's home.

There was something comforting about the Scottish knight, but she couldn't figure out why. In her short years of living in the Highlands, she'd never met a knight. Thinking about that time sent a shiver down her spine, so she took a large sip of the wine to banish the unwanted memories. Lord

Yves had exquisite taste. The drink was bold yet smooth and left warm berry flavors lingering on her tongue.

"This way," she said as she ducked around another guest and toward the door.

The knight followed. "When did ye arrive? Ye seem to ken yer way around."

His words were warm, like a blanket wrapping her in his soothing, lilting tone. She'd taken the chance on escorting him to the gardens because she honestly just wanted to listen to his deep voice.

"We arrived two days ago, so I've had time to explore."

"Who's we?" His head tilted.

"My brother and I." Their traveling group was larger than just the two of them, but that didn't seem important.

"Och, I dinnae ken yer name."

"You haven't given me yours either, sir knight." She let her regard travel to the side to meet his as she gave him an amused smile.

"'Tis Giric de Beaumont MacDonald. And I'm pleased to make yer acquaintance, fair lass."

"De Beaumont? That sounds familiar." She rolled the name over in her mind.

"'Tis the queen consort's birth name. She is my aunt."

Jennet heard the pride in his tone.

"That explains why you are trusted by King William. He is known as William the Rough, but he bears a lion on his banner. Which is it? Is he brave or ruthless?" She teased, but she was genuinely interested because she'd learned a lot about politics to help her father and Edward manage their lands.

"He can be a bit of both. A just and compassionate leader," he answered.

She knew King Richard's father, Henry II, had taken the Scottish king prisoner at one point. But that was old history, and Scotland currently had a treaty in place with King

Richard, even helping to fund the crusades. It would make sense that with Lord Yves's connections, Sir Giric would come to learn if the king's brother might be as cooperative with Scotland if the talk of rebellion was true.

They stepped out into the night air. It was refreshing, almost crisp, and if they weren't sheltered within the walls of the castle, she imagined there would be a strong breeze. It was late and the evening had grown dark, but torches lit the open space, mingling patches of light with their surroundings. The sight made her think of a childhood game where she would hop out of the shadows in an attempt to scare her father. But that was so long ago, before he became frail. Still, a lingering nostalgia inspired the magic and innocence of youth.

"What is yer name?"

"I still can't be sure it's wise to share such information with a man from Scotland."

She laughed, but it was only partly in humor. In addition to the scars she bore from her youth, she liked the idea of anonymity and being able to converse with another freely. After learning who she was, most men would progress the conversation to a topic she wasn't willing to discuss. Other barons and earls had started to question her father's absence from events. Fears of what would happen to her family should the truth get out had plagued her for years.

"If the king can trust me, I think ye can." Though his tone was playful, she thought she detected a bit of hurt pride.

"Ah, but he's your king, not mine."

She guided him to the formal garden, where the music of a minstrel floated through the air. It appeared several people had sought the beauty of the flowers and a view of the stars. Under one of the torches, a group of people gathered, listening to the strains of music. She found herself not wanting to share her knight's company with others.

"Do ye trust Lord Yves's judgment? He believed me safe enough to invite me into his home."

"I'm not sure his assessment is sound. After all, it appears half of England is present."

"So 'tis no' only my country ye disparage?" He laughed. The hearty sound was pleasing, and she found herself wanting to hear it again.

"I spread my distrust fairly. This way." She motioned to a secluded spot where, although it was darker, she knew there was a bench. She'd sat on it yesterday and studied the design of the garden.

She eased onto the solid wood, and he followed. "Ye have made it a challenge for me to earn yer favor."

"Then perhaps you might wish to rethink your participation in the jousts."

"Nae. I'm here for the melee." His regard seemed to drift then as if he were trying to decide what flower was on the rose bush.

"Then how are you to know you have earned my trust if I can't bestow a gift upon you?" What if he had interest in a different lass? "Unless there is another lady you wish to woo?" She held her breath, waiting for a reply.

His attention returned. "My thoughts have been on other concerns. I've never sought the favor of a lass, but ye are convincing me that perhaps 'tis time I change my ways."

She took a sip of wine and was thankful the dimness of the evening had wrapped the castle grounds in its embrace. Surely her cheeks had pinkened with the heat that crept up her neck. It wasn't so much his words or the thought of the flirtation she'd started, but because it was not typical of her to be so bold.

He was easy to talk to, and she found their conversation flowed as readily as the wine at the feast. Words were leaving her mouth before she could collect her typical reserve. Perhaps it was that he didn't know her family or that he'd seen her with her bow and not judged her. The anonymity afforded her freedom she'd never had.

"Giric." She liked the sound of his name. "What do you think of a woman who sneaks away from the crowd to practice archery? Most men frown upon it."

"I find it intriguing. Ye had great form, and ye seem to have an ability with it. 'Tis a skill many men even struggle with and something ye should be proud of."

She thought she heard true admiration in his words.

"You are trying very hard to earn that favor."

"Is it working?" His smile was genuine; his straight white teeth almost gleaming through the shadows.

"Ye may have to take up a lance to find out," she challenged.

A burst of laughter from the assembled crowd broke through the air. Her gaze moved that way, finding Eddie and Ada had joined the revelry. He would put a guard on her if he found her alone like this on a secluded bench with a man. She needed to escape before he saw her. Despite connecting for the first time ever with a man in a way that made her want to linger, Jennet stood to leave.

"I must retire for the evening."

He rose. "Can I escort ye back to yer... Are ye here in the caste or lodging elsewhere?"

She left the question unanswered as she caught the movement of the crowd starting to disperse. "I must go. I know my way. Thank you for the conversation, Sir Giric."

His regard turned to the crowd, then to her. "At least honor me with yer name."

"You have made progress, sir knight, and though I have enjoyed your company, I still don't trust so easily."

She thought he would protest, but something stole his attention. When he stiffened, she took the opportunity to move farther into the shadows and toward the interior of the castle. "Have a good evening, Sir Giric."

"Where will I find ye?" he asked, only giving her half of his attention.

"I'll be touring the village tomorrow, and then ye will find me watching the jousts."

His face darkened toward whatever he was studying, but he nodded. She turned and rushed through the yard before her brother could see her. Anticipation shot through her at the thought that the comely knight might seek her out tomorrow.

CHAPTER 3

$\mathcal{G}$iric restrained the need to chase after the lass, see her safely to wherever she was staying, and steal a few more moments with her. He'd never felt such ease with a woman. Her levity had given him a reprieve from the anger and anxiety that had plagued his thoughts since the start of this journey.

If his enemy's son hadn't appeared across the garden, he would have insisted on escorting her, but he'd waited eleven years for this opportunity, and he couldn't squander it because he found an English lass intriguing. After the melee, perhaps he would seek her out, but until he found justice, he couldn't let his guard down.

He stood and moved through the shadows to observe Edward Linton as he laughed and smiled at a lass by his side. He still couldn't see the lady's face because the cloth from her headdress shielded her, but her identity didn't matter. He focused on his target. They strolled in the direction his little archer had traveled. Taking up position behind them, he followed.

Edward had a slight limp, but it wasn't enough to make him stand out. It might, however, be a weakness he could exploit. The Englishman was almost as tall as him but thinner, muscular. He would be a formidable foe, so Giric needed to keep in mind that his victory was not guaranteed.

All the more reason not to get involved with the alluring, quick-witted lass who'd just sprinted away from him without giving her name. While he lurked behind the unsuspecting pair as they walked back to the castle, he banished thoughts of the bonny Sassenach and brought back the memories that would clarify his task.

The day that his world was destroyed had been much like this one. He remembered the warmth of the brightly shining sun and relived one of the scenes that taunted him.

When he'd come upon the inn, a young child had stood alone in the small clearing behind the aging wooden building, aiming arrows at a makeshift target on a tree. The bow had been twice the size of what a lad should have. Giric had been drawn to the child's poise, so he'd stood at the fringe of the forest to watch the boy with chopped, dirty-brown hair. After he'd made the first few shots, Giric had become mesmerized by the lad's form and skill.

After a few moments, though, he'd snuck away and gone into the structure to deliver the letter his father had instructed him to give the innkeeper. The man wore a scowl and only grunted when he'd handed over the note.

"Does he want a response straight away?"

Giric nodded. "Aye. He told me to wait."

"Take a seat." The man grunted and walked away.

While the innkeeper was in a back room, the boy with the bow slinked in through the front door, shutting it quietly. Only it wasn't a lad. Glancing at the wee thing, Giric saw that while she was dressed as a boy and her hair had been shorn to hide her femininity, she had gentle cheekbones and rosy cheeks.

When the lass spotted him, she hid her face and darted for the stairs.

Just then, the innkeeper returned and barked, "What are ye doing out here?"

"I'm sorry," she broke off as her wide eyes shifted toward him then back to the man before she continued uncertainly, "Father."

"I told you not to go out there again." He stomped across the room, took the child's bow, and tossed it into a corner, then his hand smacked across the girl's cheek. She fell to the floor and began to quiver.

Jumping up, Giric rushed to her side. He held out a hand to help the lass, but she shied away. Taking her trembling fingers anyway, he drew her to her feet.

"Stay out of this, boy. 'Tis none of your concern," the innkeeper snapped.

"Ye shouldnae be striking her like that." He glanced at the lass, but her face was averted despite the grip of her hand clinging to his.

"Neither you nor your father can tell me what to do in my own home," the man spat at him.

The fingers in his squirmed and pulled free. The wee thing stood tall but didn't meet his gaze. "Go," she whispered. "I'll be all right."

Turning to face her, he tilted her chin up, but she wouldn't meet his eyes.

"Here's your father's answer. Now get out of here, boy." The innkeeper handed him a letter and pushed him toward the door, shoving him out. A crack sounded with the slamming of the portal, and a bolt clicked into place, then angry, jumbled words he couldn't make out filtered from under the thick, wooden plank.

He'd run to get his father.

Before the rest of the memory could intrude, Giric was back in the present and nearing his bedchamber. Edward and his companion were just a few doors down. The Englishman opened one, and the pair disappeared inside. Giric furtively counted only five doors from his own. That would make it easy to keep an eye on his target.

He slipped inside his room, then bolted the door and paced as he undressed. His original intent on this trip was to end Baron Gillingham's life with honor on the melee field. But in addition to taking his father from him all those years ago, with his absence, the man had denied him that opportunity as well.

He couldn't take Edward's life without knowing the man —after all, he was probably just a child when the baron had murdered Giric's father. The son was not responsible for his father's sins unless he knew about them and had done nothing to seek justice.

He would just have to capture Edward during the melee. Then he could question the man and use him as ransom if necessary to get his true enemy here. And if the baron's son was aware of his father's misdeeds and had done nothing to atone for them, Giric might just take his life instead.

Wouldn't that cause more damage to the baron, anyway? Ending Edward's life would surely destroy the man, and wouldn't that be a more fitting way to avenge his father's death?

～

Early the next morning before the sun had a chance to rise, Giric made his way to the great hall in hope that Edward would make an appearance to break his fast. Sleep had eluded him until he'd decided to follow the baron's son as time allowed to get to know the man's strengths and weaknesses. His years at court had taught him how to observe others without their knowledge.

Just as golden rays broke through the windows, Edward strolled into the hall and sat near a group of men who welcomed him with boisterous greetings that Giric could see, but not hear, from his seat. The group ate as they laughed and talked with one another.

When they finished their meal, Edward stood and started back toward the steps, but one of the men he'd been dining with stopped him, then herded him toward the exit.

Giric covertly followed the pair as they left the castle and walked through the village. They wandered in and out of establishments and stopped to converse with a couple of knights on the street. Giric watched as the tall, thin, blond man with Edward seemed to orchestrate their interaction with the others. He comported himself as if he were in charge, and Edward's easy smile made it appear as if they might be close friends. Giric would find out who he was by the time the sun set.

A soft, familiar laugh danced above the sound of the busy street, floating through the air and resting gently in his ears. A small thrill shot through him. He turned and scoured the crowds.

There she was. His bonny lass from last night.

She wore her curly, waist-length hair partially plaited and free of a headpiece today. It was the first time he could see her lovely, oval-shaped face without any barriers. He was better able to appreciate her beauty this way. The day was sunny, and the warm rays highlighted the changing shades of her tresses. The glorious strands were a subtle brown, but at the same time, it had a luminescent quality to it as if the sun had kissed it.

He liked the idea that she might be partial to being out in nature. He had assumed English lasses spent all their time indoors mending stockings.

She had high cheekbones that were rosy with mirth as she watched a show where the actors were using dolls to mimic the characters they were portraying. He had to admit it was entertaining, but he was more interested in watching her. He could become accustomed to gazing upon the lady's face.

It was a shame she was from England, and he did not have time to court her properly due to his mission. He had learned a little about her, though. Her clothing, like today's purple gown, made it obvious she was no camp follower. She seemed to be a lady of some gentler breeding, perhaps the daughter of a knight or lord.

He tore his gaze away to watch the door of the shop Edward had entered. As he waited for his quarry to reemerge, he pondered the commonality of the man's name. He'd met two more Edwards this morning while breaking his fast.

The lass laughed, drawing his attention again, and he couldn't resist moving closer. Although his feet carried him toward her, his eyes darted back and forth between the English lass and the door to the establishment where Edward was shopping.

He found himself by her side. "Good day to ye, fair lass."

Her eyes met his and lit. "Good day, Sir Giric. I see you have found me."

"At first I thought 'twould be hard no' kenning yer name, but all I had to do was ask any passersby where to find the bonniest lass in all of England."

She blushed, and two women standing near her broke out into laughter.

"I trust you slept well and are rested for the day's activities," she said.

A loud burst of noise came from the stage, and the other ladies returned their attention to the show, but his lass kept her focus fixed on him.

"I might have slept better had I no' thought there was a lass whose favor I wish to gain but who willnae grace me with her name." He moved close and whispered in her ear, "If I ask yer friends, will they tell me?"

But he didn't want that; he wanted her to open up to him, and he desired to hear it from her mouth. His eyes were drawn to her lips. They were full and smiling and a deep, rosy pink that he suddenly realized he wanted to taste.

He swallowed as unexpected stirrings shot through him.

"I have known you one evening. They are faithful companions who have earned my trust over many years, and I believe they will keep my secret should you compel me to ask them to do so."

"I wouldnae dream of forcing yer hand in any matter. Surrender is sweeter when given freely."

"Well, then." She leaned in, and he caught a whiff of fresh-cut roses. He wanted to close the distance between them and inhale. There was something intoxicating about this woman. He'd never had someone so boldly taunt him. "Ye have just earned a point for your honesty."

He licked his lips, and she drew back. Her intense gaze locked on his, tightening his body.

"I am making it my quest to earn yer confidence." Her friends were watching them again with sly smiles, and he knew they'd overheard. He nodded in their direction, waiting for his lady, if he could call her that when he didn't know her name, to introduce them.

"Then perhaps ye will escort us to the bakery when the show is done. I have heard they make the most divine lemon cakes."

His gut twisted. Argh, he wanted to. But he had his mission. His gaze darted back to the shop, just in time to see Edward strolling away from it. If he'd waited a second longer, he would have missed the man.

"I'm devastated that I cannae join ye. I have some business to see to." His attention jumped between Edward and the lass. He would lose the man in a moment if he didn't leave. Yet his English lady looked disappointed, and regret stabbed in his chest. Had he just destroyed his chances of getting to know her?

"Perhaps I will see ye this afternoon? Ye said ye would be attending the jousts," he said as he backed away.

"Yes. I will." Her tone was optimistic, and relief filled him when he realized she did not feel slighted by his refusal to escort them.

"Then do I have yer permission to seek ye out?" He took her hand, surprised by his own action. She didn't protest.

"I would enjoy that, Sir Giric."

He liked the sound of his name on her lips and the feel of her soft skin touching his.

"Farewell, my nameless lady." He brought her hand to his lips as he dipped his head. Before placing his mouth to her flesh, he inhaled. This time along with the roses, he smelled sandalwood. His whole body tensed at the intoxicating mix, and he wanted to pull her near, close the distance between them, and...

What? They didn't know each other. Nothing would come from this flirtation, but he couldn't stop.

He pressed his mouth to her soft skin. His gaze lifted to see her eyes transfixed on him. Her lips were parted, and he wondered what it would be like to kiss her. If just skimming her hand set his body on end, what would the sensation of her wine-kissed mouth do to his control?

He pulled away. "Until then, fair lass." He bowed, turned, and regretfully ran in the direction Edward had gone.

~

Jennet studied Giric's broad back and shoulders as he bounded down the street. In the dim candlelit rooms and courtyards of last eve, she'd not realized how light his hair was. With his build and coloring, he could be a descendant of Thor from the famed Old Norse myth. And she did feel as if a bolt of lightning had jolted her because her chest was light as exhilaration thrummed through her.

Ada tugged at her hand and drew Jennet's attention back to her friends. Her cheeks heated as both her companions waited for her to explain her flirtation with the stranger. Warmth spread through her limbs as she tried to contain her excitement. Was the knight truly vying for her affections?

"Who was that?" Ada's smile accused her of hiding the brawny man.

Well, she had. She'd wanted to keep her Scottish knight a secret, and she'd thought after last night, she might never see him again anyway. Besides, her best friend had been absent all evening, and she could only guess by Ada's flushed cheeks and disheveled appearance when she'd arrived at their room this morning that she and Eddie had been celebrating their engagement ahead of their wedding.

"His name is Sir Giric de Beaumont MacDonald."

"And?" Ada prodded.

"And he's the nephew of the queen consort of Scotland." She had to admit that the tingles spreading through her just talking about him were a warning sign that perhaps she liked the knight's attention a bit more than prudent.

"Where did you meet him?" Her friend tapped her foot.

"We shared a dance last evening."

"And you were going to keep him a secret?" Ada pinched her lips together in mock disapproval.

"Well, you were quite busy with my brother last night, and I couldn't find Sybil, so I hadn't had the chance to tell you."

Sybil stilled and became stoic.

Ada had been beaming and talkative all morning, but their other companion and chamber-mate, Sybil, had been appalled by Ada and Eddie's actions. Sybil's brother was the Earl of Bruton, Lord Roger Nash. They were close neighbors in the south and had accompanied them on the journey. Sybil was sharing a room with her and Ada since half of England seemed to have been invited to this tournament.

Over the last few years, Sybil and the baron had been visiting sporadically, and Jennet sometimes found herself alone with the baron as her friend had tried to steal Edward's affections. Lord Roger Nash was close to fifteen years her senior, and she was always intimidated by the way he took charge of their household, ordering everyone about as if their servants belonged to him. She tolerated it because he'd been a good friend and mentor to Eddie. Although she loved Ada and thought she was the best choice for Edward, Jennet couldn't help but feel a bit of compassion for Sybil's hurt pride at Eddie's disinterest.

"Well, tell us all about this Scottish knight," Ada persisted.

"We only shared a dance and conversation."

"It appears he wishes to share more than a dance with you. Do I need to tell Edward to beware of Scottish knights, lest the man whisk you away, and I never see you again?" Ada giggled, but Sybil only narrowed her eyes.

Heat crept up Jennet's neck. "No. You know how I feel about Scotland. You will never find me living there again."

"As long as you promise not to leave me. Let's get those pastries. Sybil, what did you think of the show?" Ada turned to their friend, trying to pull her into the conversation. Maybe she sensed the tension as well.

"It was a nice distraction, but I'm looking forward to the jousts." Sybil finally smiled, and Jennet hoped the animosity she'd felt after learning Edward would marry Ada was melting.

"Perhaps we will find you a knight or a baron. Have you spied anyone who might catch your interest?" Maybe now Sybil could focus on another man. Perhaps Jennet's younger brother, William, who had remained at home to see to their father. Yes, if she couldn't find Sybil a suitor here, William would do. That way, they could all remain close.

"No. Not yet, but we have plenty of time." Sybil started toward the shop.

Jennet and Ada followed as they made their way to the bakery. They'd almost reached it when shouting erupted behind them. Jennet turned and saw a horde of people running in their direction. A woman fleeing the raucous crowd smacked into her, knocking her to the ground. Ada held out a hand as people continued to dash away from the scene.

On her feet, Jennet glanced around to see people streaming toward them. Sybil shouted, "Over here," and motioned toward the buildings.

She and Ada ran for the small alley between two establishments where their friend waited. Jennet's eyes darting around as if she expected more danger. It appeared they would be safe from the fleeing villagers and visitors until whatever had happened to upset the crowd was settled.

Her hands burned, and she lifted them to inspect her trembling palms. Red marks evinced her fall, but the skin was not torn.

"Are you hurt?" Ada asked.

"No. I'll just be bruised. I wonder what's happening." They moved deeper into the alleyway.

Taking a deep breath, Jennet turned to look back toward the street and froze. A large man blocked the way they'd come in. Her pulse accelerated. He brandished a knife, and his gaze darted back and forth between the three of them as he slowly stalked forward, swinging the blade around as if trying to choose who to attack first. The dark intent in his gaze sent chills spiraling to the pit of her stomach.

Sybil grabbed her arm and pulled her farther back, attempting to shield her from the approaching man. She glanced over her shoulder to the rear of the close. Their escape was cut off by large wooden crates that had been left outside one of the business's doors. She swung around. The brute had turned his sights on Ada.

The man started toward her brother's love, who stood shaking and rooted to the ground. Jennet pulled free from Sybil's grasp and latched onto Ada to draw her back before the man got closer.

"What's happening here?" A familiar voice came from behind their attacker, but the drawl was sharp, angry.

Sir Giric.

Relief flooded her.

The brute turned to face the knight who had come to their rescue. Without a word, the villain charged at their savior, attempting to sink his knife into the Scottish knight's side. Giric dodged, and the man stumbled past him, nearly falling to the ground. The brute regained his footing and charged at Sir Giric again, but her knight knocked the weapon free of the man's hand, then punched their attacker in the face. The brute's hand rose to his nose as crimson spilled from his nostrils. The man's eyes narrowed with rage before he reevaluated his opponent and fled down the alley for the street.

Sir Giric gave chase.

He stopped at the street and gazed in the direction the man had run. But he shook his head before pivoting around and running toward them. "He's lost in the crowd. I willnae be able to find him right now. I'll make inquiries this afternoon."

All she could do was nod.

"Are ye injured?" He took her hand and lifted it to inspect for damage before his scrutiny traveled over her, seeming to check for injuries. She turned her fingers over in his palm and twined them with his, reassuring herself with his steadying presence. His hand in hers was comforting, and she would hold on as long as he let her.

The concern in his eyes surrounded her with warmth. She fought the urge to throw herself into his embrace until the pounding in her heart stilled. His strong arms would surely stop this quaking in her core.

"No. You arrived before he was able to cause harm. I think he was crazed. It looked like he was going to kill us."

Giric's gaze traveled to her companions to evaluate their condition as well. "Are ye ladies uninjured?"

Her friends only nodded. Apparently satisfied everyone was safe, he analyzed their surroundings.

"This way," he instructed as he guided them out the back of the alley through a space that she hadn't seen before. She was thankful his hand still held hers. Several people loitered on this roadway, but it was calm.

Giric stopped and glanced around; she assumed to get their bearings. "There appears to have been a brawl. I think Lord Yves is having the streets cleared. Hopefully, that will end whatever foolishness has taken place."

"Do ye think it's s-s-safe?" Ada stumbled over the words. It was the first time in years her friend's stutter had been noticeable, and Jennet's heart ached for her.

"Aye. I'll see ye ladies back to the castle. Come." He looked them all over before his gaze again rested on her, reassuring, soothing. He stopped. "Is that where ye are staying?"

"Yes. The castle."

"Then come, my lady." He kept his hand locked securely with hers.

"Jennet," she said.

Their eyes met, and she felt as if she were floating. For a long moment, they were the only people in the world. She licked her lips as her body heated. His touch and the intensity of his blue gaze sent a rush of awareness through her.

"My name is Jennet."

CHAPTER 4

*G*iric turned the word over in his mind. *Jennet.* It was a lovely name. It suited her. He was frozen, gazing into eyes that watched him as if he could save her from drowning.

Instead, he was falling into the dark pools of her eyes. She trusted him. Delight shot through him. Despite her teasing from the evening before, he sensed she was reserved and didn't take many into her confidence.

A pressure somewhere in his chest lightened. He'd been blaming himself for his father's fate for years. And now this lass gazed upon him as if he had a purpose. One that years of fighting under the king had not given him, something deeper than duty.

A kiss from her was more necessary than a breath.

He shook his head. This was not why he was here. He'd come to England to find revenge, not be sidetracked by this bonny creature. Aye, she made him laugh, but she also made him forget everything else.

Och, where was his enemy's son now?

He'd lost the man in the confusion. When shouts had started, and the throng of people began running, he'd seen her…Jennet…across the street as her friend pulled her from the ground. They'd sought shelter in the alley. He'd dodged the currents to reach her and ensure she made it to safety.

Even now, as her hand trembled in his, he felt a strong urge to protect her. Maybe it was because he'd failed so long ago. But he didn't think so—there was something about this woman that reached in and soothed the scorched parts of his being that he'd thought would never bear emotion again.

Perhaps he should get to know her better. He'd never had such a reaction to a lass. His hand tingled where it touched hers, and he found it nearly impossible to release his hold.

Once they'd emerged onto the new street, he swallowed. "Did any of ye recognize the man?" he asked.

"No. I've never seen him," Jennet said, then looked to her friends for their reactions. The brunette shook her head, and the blonde bit her lip then looked away as if she were trying to block out the memory.

"Did he say what he wanted?"

Jennet shook her head. "He did not say a word."

Unease crept in. It was odd that the man hadn't demanded coin or something else that the ladies were unwilling to give. The attacker had seemed coherent and steady on his feet, so Giric doubted he was a madman or a drunk.

The brunette glanced his way. "We are fortunate you were nearby. Thank you, Sir Giric."

He nodded. "I only wish I could have detained him."

"Ah, forgive me," Jennet said. "This is Ada Ward. She'll soon be wed to my brother. And this"—she smiled toward the blonde—"is Sybil Nash. A close neighbor and friend. Her brother is the Earl of Bruton."

"'Tis a pleasure to meet ye both." He bowed, not releasing Jennet's hand.

"Will you be in the joust today, Sir Giric? Both my brother and Jennet's will be." Sybil smiled, but her attention still darted around, possibly worried they hadn't seen the last of their attacker.

"Nae. There is another knight here to represent King William in the jousting tourney."

"We will be watching from the stands. Will you be coming to observe?" Ada grinned but judging by the raised eyebrow, she teased Jennet as much as she was asking after his whereabouts.

Jennet's cheeks were flushed when she peeked up at him. And for a moment, he wished he could join them.

"I dinnae ken if I will attend. I hear Lady Jennet doesnae offer knights her favor, and my pride might be damaged irreparably if I put myself in a position for failure." His free hand covered his heart.

She smiled then, a playful, private grin meant only for him, and a thrill shot down his spine at the knowledge that they shared a secret.

"I'm sure she might break with tradition to honor one who saved her life and that of her friends." Ada laughed.

"Are ye willing to do such a thing, lass?" His voice was rough, and somehow it felt like he was asking for more.

"How am I to bestow such an offering if you are not fighting?" Jennet replied, a teasing note giving her voice a lightness that he was happy to hear after the scare they had just experienced. Their friend, Sybil, was quiet and appeared as if she'd not yet recovered from their ordeal.

"I will be participating in the melee if the lady chooses to honor me."

"You prefer hand-to-hand combat?" Jennet glanced at him, her brown gaze trapping him along with the playful tone she'd possessed last evening.

"I prefer being close enough to see my opponent quiver, no matter the sport." His thumb brushed up and down on her soft skin.

Her breath caught, and he was enthralled by the way her

mouth fell open as if she would welcome a kiss. Her tongue darted across her lips and desire shot through him. Och, this reaction was new to him. The world around them disappeared as their eyes locked.

A voice cleared to garner their attention...the blonde, Sybil. "We should probably be on our way back. I don't want to miss our brothers in the parade of knights."

Pulling his gaze from Jennet, he examined the area and realized they'd not moved. The baron's men appeared to be clearing the remaining visitors from the street. He should escort the ladies to the castle, and then he would double back to see if he could find any clues to the assailant's identity. He'd managed to get a good look at the man, and perhaps he would find someone who knew him.

They started toward the castle. "And do ye have a knight that ye favor, Lady Sybil?" he asked.

Her lips pinched together. "No, I do not." She picked up her pace and set out in front of them. Ada followed her. Although it appeared that he'd broached a sensitive subject, he was glad, for the slower pace Jennet kept beside him. He enjoyed being the object of her attention.

She leaned in, and he inhaled the heady combination of rose and sandalwood. "Perhaps you may help us find someone worthy of Sybil's interest. Ada stole my brother's affections before Sybil had the chance."

"I would like to meet yer brother. Perhaps he could give me insight on how to woo his sister." He was surprised at how his jesting words settled in his chest and became something more than what he had intended.

"I think you are better at it than you believe."

"Why are ye no' wed?" He couldn't imagine the men in England not tripping over themselves to ask for her hand.

"My mother passed when I was young, and I eventually took over caring for the men in my life. My brothers are younger than I, and until Eddie takes the helm of the family, they need me."

It was the first mention of her brother's name. He must be another Edward—och, the English were so predictable. At least this one went by a shortened version.

"What of yer father?"

Jennet's gaze turned down before glancing back up at him. She seemed to be collecting her thoughts. "He has been ill for some time."

He'd upset her. Giric wanted to bring her smile back, but he didn't know what to say. Instead, he attempted to give her a reassuring nod.

"It was especially bad when Eddie's horse fell on his leg. I think he would have taken on the responsibilities and married Ada sooner, had he not had to use the time to recover. It won't be long now."

"And will yer brother find ye a husband?" Tension wound around his shoulders as he waited for her response, unaccountably worried that her life might already be plotted for her.

"No. I shall be allowed the freedom to find my own if I desire one."

His feet stalled, and his breath caught. Might she choose him? He'd not really thought until this moment that there could truly be more between them. The prospect sent a thrill through him, but he had other priorities that came first.

∼

Jennet was surprised when Giric stopped. Glancing up at him, she knew the emotion he wore on his face. It was shock. "Does it surprise you that a daughter of a baron might be able to choose who she weds?"

"Until this moment, ye could have been the daughter of a

miller for all I kenned." He grinned, and it was endearing. One side of his mouth rose a little higher than the other, and his blue gaze sparked with amusement. "But, aye, I would think yer family might be concerned over connections to match yer station."

"My parents endured hardships for that very reason and swore they would not force their children to make a choice not based on mutual affection."

"That is uncommon for the barons of England. I'd thought them all cold and heartless." His brows knit together, and his eyes darkened as if he was speaking from some experience.

"Are you going to join us?" Ada's voice reached her, and she realized they'd fallen a bit behind. They continued to stroll toward the castle.

Perhaps she was telling him too much, but she found it easy to speak to Sir Giric. "My mother was betrothed to another before my father had the chance to ask for her hand. At the time, my father was the third of three sons, and it was his eldest brother that my mother was promised to."

"That does seem like a horrible twist of fate."

"They couldn't bear to be parted, so he stole her from my uncle."

"How brave of them to risk losing so much."

"They lost much more than you could imagine, and because of it, my parents swore they would let their children choose their own mates." As she shared words that she'd never volunteered to others, not even Ada and Sybil, a pressure evaporated from her chest.

"Ye have me curious to hear more of their tale." Giric's inquisitive stare met hers, begging for more of the story.

Maybe she'd needed someone to talk to after hiding her father's illness and the events that led up to it for so long. Still, the next part of her story woke her on too many nights. It might be a relief to tell this man what had happened to her, but she would wait until she'd had a glass of wine to fortify her nerves.

They'd reached the castle. She still held Giric's hand and found she had not the will to pull her fingers away. It may not be appropriate considering they barely knew each other, but his comforting presence had kept her grounded after the attack.

She was growing fond of this Scottish knight, and that was a problem. Scotland held nothing but horrible memories for her and her family. If she were to encourage Sir Giric's attention, she should not flaunt it in front of anyone who might tell Eddie until she'd had the opportunity to speak with him. And she was not ready for her brother to know she was becoming enthralled by someone who was at the tourney on King William's behalf.

They needed to part ways here, before her brother might see them.

"Perhaps, Sir Giric, if you find me this evening, I will share their fate."

"I would be honored."

"After tonight's feast, shall we meet in the gardens? At the same bench, perhaps?" Anticipation was already coursing through her at the thought of sitting alone in their secret spot.

"Aye. I will count the minutes till 'tis time."

Her chest pounded at his words and the thought that he might be as enthralled with her as she was him. His eyes had an intensity to them that they hadn't previously held, and she thought he might try to kiss her. She wanted him to. She had her freedom now and could make her own choices—why shouldn't she? Chest tightening, her lips parted, and her chin tilted up, but he did not move to further their connection.

Her breath quickened as they stood motionless, hands still twined. Her breasts were heavy with tension and antici-pation, but he only continued to stare into her eyes. Had she misread what she'd thought to be genuine interest? Feeling her skin flush as heat moved through her, she swallowed and drew back her shoulders.

Perhaps he'd not moved in because they were on a busy thoroughfare. It would be like what she'd learned of him thus far to protect her honor.

"Thank you, Sir Giric." She drew her hand back, managing to release her hold on him and the words despite the lump in her throat. She gave a small curtsey and inched backward.

He blinked, and his shoulders dipped as if he'd been surprised by her abrupt retreat. "What have I done?"

"You possibly saved my life and that of my friends." She smiled.

He took a deep breath and nodded, the confusion in his gaze retreating. "I am happy to have been nearby."

"I look forward to seeing you this evening."

"And I as well, Lady Jennet." He backed and bowed, then he turned and strode again toward the village.

As Jennet rejoined her friends, Sybil's scrutiny pinned her. "Are you sure you know what you're doing? He looks as if he's quite interested in you and he's from Scotland. Your brother might not approve."

"I know. There is no harm in talking to him, and he just saved us." But she knew she was wrong about the lack of harm. She already missed the warmth of his steady hand, and her heart beat with eagerness as she thought of seeing him this evening.

If she let this go further, Eddie would have to be notified. He'd always agreed she could make her own choice, but none of them had ever considered she might go back to the place that held such pain for her family. Logic had always kept her safe, but this time, she just couldn't obey the warning signals in her head.

CHAPTER 5

*J*ennet and her friends returned to their room to allow their nerves to calm a bit more. When Sybil's hands had finally stopped trembling after a short rest, they had given in to Ada's demands to attend the festivities. Jennet was keen on seeing her brother in the parade of knights and grew impatient as they made their way to the jousting fields.

By the time they'd arrived, the parade was almost over, and they'd missed both Eddie's and Lord Roger's introductions. The raised viewing stand afforded a nice perspective of the jousting fields. Mounted knights trotted across the field as a man called out who the next participant was and where he hailed from. Cheers rang out as each name was called, and the men took up their starting positions.

She'd seen the knights here the last couple days, practicing and preparing for the tournament events. Brown patches of earth showed the turf was already pounded flat from their efforts. She found herself scanning the crowds, looking for her Scottish savior.

Why had Giric been sent if the king had chosen another to represent him in the tourney? Perhaps just for the melee, but she didn't know enough about the politics of tournaments to judge. Frankly, after Eddie's accident, competition on horseback frightened her. She was glad Giric had chosen not to take the field. It would be hard enough to watch her brother.

Did she even care why Giric was here? Only that he was, and her heart skipped a beat as she thought of seeing him this evening. Never before had she been so intrigued by someone, and his humor matched her own. Other than Ada and Sybil, she'd not laughed with anyone since her youth was stolen. For the first time in years, in his presence, she felt alive and free.

And she'd never wanted to kiss a man before, but his gentle hand in hers had sent gooseflesh trailing up her arms. The way he'd gazed into her eyes had awoken something in her that had lain in wait for his smile. Perhaps...she felt the warmth creep up her cheeks...he would put his lips to hers as they sat on their hidden bench this evening.

Her core vibrated with something new, a rush she didn't expect, and it sent heat to the spot between her thighs. Oh, she mused, this must be desire. Even the thought of him made her body thrum to life in ways foreign to her. And despite her past in Scotland, she might consider traveling there again. Perhaps all Scots weren't barbarians. She wanted to know more about Giric, and that might mean understanding his homeland.

Ada broke into her thoughts. "They're arguing again. I feel so awful for her."

She hoped her friend couldn't tell where her thoughts had been. "Who?" she asked.

"Sybil and Lord Roger." Ada pointed, and Jennet craned backward to observe the pair who glared at each other behind the stands.

"I didn't know he'd stopped her as we entered. We must have missed him parade across the field."

Sybil's fists were clenched at her sides. Perhaps she was starting to stand up for herself. Lord Roger seemed to enjoy controlling everyone around him. Her heart ached for how hard life must be for Sybil.

Jennet shook her head. "I think we need to find her a husband so that she'll no longer be under his command." After what her uncle had done to her, she could never live in such a powerless environment again. She craved the freedom to make her own decisions.

"I agree. Perhaps some champion will stand out today, and then we can sing of her merits to him." Ada laughed.

Jennet giggled and said, "He'll be in love before we ever introduce them."

Ada perked up. Her attention pulled to the front of the stands. "Oh, there's Edward. He looks magnificent."

Her heart warmed as her best friend's eyes shone with pride and love. They deserved each other. But what of her? Jennet had never taken the time to discover what she might find attractive in a man. Sir Giric's laughter floated in her mind. He was kind and amusing...and pleasing to gaze upon.

Her cheeks once again heated. "Do you think Eddie would truly not be pleased if I wanted to know Sir Giric better?"

"I think if the knight is worthy of his sister's affections, he will give the man a chance despite his allegiance to King William."

Jennet smiled.

"And he may have saved our lives. I'm sure Edward would feel some gratitude toward him," Ada continued.

Jennet's eyes stung. It seemed childish, but her friend's approval was important. She was in a place she didn't understand. "Do you think I am foolish for hoping Sir Giric desires me?"

"No, I do not."

"My heart patters so when he's near, and all I can think of is seeing him again. Is that wrong?"

"No. 'Tis proof that you were destined to be together. I felt the same way about your brother when we first met."

"But we were just children then. You've had time to learn who he is."

"Aye, but my heart knew the first time I saw him. It was my mind that had to catch up. You only have a few days. I suggest you get to know him."

Jennet felt heat creep up her neck because that was exactly what she wanted to do.

Ada smiled. "If you decide he is the right one for you, I will talk to your brother."

She threw her arms around Ada. She knew if she decided Giric was her choice and if both she and Ada asked Eddie, he wouldn't be able to refuse them.

Sybil appeared by their side. "Did I miss something?"

"No. We're just so happy to be here. What was going on with your brother?"

"Just his usual demands. Oh, and Jennet, he wishes for you to share a dance with him this evening after the feast."

Her mouth fell open. Lord Roger had never shown interest in her other than ordering her around when he'd visited her brother. If he'd not served as a mentor and friend to Eddie all these years, she would probably have denied the overbearing tyrant admittance into their home. She only put up with him for Eddie and Sybil's sakes.

Before she could continue, Sybil frowned. Jennet followed her gaze to see Edward at the box's edge, Ada giving him a kerchief. Happiness washed over her for them, but then dread as she remembered Eddie's injury.

"Jennet," Sybil's angry tone broke in.

"Aye." She turned back to the woman.

"I said, 'I'm going to our chamber to rest. My head aches.'"

"Oh. You'll miss the jousting."

Sybil's gaze darted to Ada and Eddie behind her. "I think I need the rest right now."

"All right, then. We will see you before tonight's feast."

"Yes." Sybil was turning and rushing away before she could say another word. Perhaps it was best she didn't watch Ada's reaction to Eddie on the field today.

Then Jennet was alone, and her mind drifted to where Sir Giric might be just now and if he was thinking of her.

~

Giric's attention roamed the great hall, hoping to catch a glimpse of Lady Jennet. Tonight's feast was only for the guests who were staying in the castle, and he was pleased that he now knew she could make an appearance.

The meal was not yet over, and by virtue of making the acquaintance of Lord Marcus Debar, Lord Yves's guest of honor, Giric had gained a seat near their host. Although the conversation had been lively, it had never turned to politics, and he'd not learned anything about where Lord Yves's loyalties lay. Fortunately, he was now a step closer toward attaining an audience with their host. It would be easier to bring up more sensitive matters when the man thought the topic was casual. At least he'd made some progress on that mission.

He'd spent part of the afternoon scouring the village in hopes of finding the arse who had attacked the ladies today. What he'd learned was disturbing, and it made him anxious that he'd not yet seen any of the ladies tonight during the meal.

The rest of the afternoon, he'd spent exploring the camp and sparring with Sir Thomas Brisbois of Kelso. Giric had never met him before today and had only heard of the man who had been put in King William's prison for treason. It was said that Sir Thomas had never been defeated in battle or on the field of honor.

Giric wasn't sure why his king had plucked the knight from prison and sent him to the tourney, but it wasn't his place to question his king. It had been a nice diversion to practice with a fellow Scot this afternoon and to train in hand-to-hand combat with the tall, dark-haired man in the lists, especially since fighting against one so capable proved that he was ready for his mission in the melee.

Throughout the day, he'd also scanned the crowd, looking for Edward Linton, but had no luck with that pursuit. Should he approach Edward before the melee to get information from him or wait until he'd taken the man on the field of battle?

Though the melee was only a practice exercise for battle, real weapons were used, and it was permitted to take prisoners and ask a ransom for their return. Would Edward's family present him with the devil who'd killed his father if he demanded it? That was his hope.

The final course was being served, but Giric excused himself, knowing he would get no further with the baron tonight and that Edward was missing. He had another diversion in mind.

Really, she'd been in his thoughts all afternoon. Meandering out to the gardens, he took a seat on the bench by the roses, waiting for the most intriguing lass in all of England to make an appearance.

Thick tapers lit the doorway to the courtyard, and as Jennet appeared in the glowing light, his breath caught. A rush of desire and something deeper erupted from his core.

Could he have come to England for vengeance only to find something more? The companionship he'd felt with her was like nothing he'd experienced with any other lass. He could imagine sharing his darkest moments and fears with her and her response making him laugh, or her arms holding him tightly in a comforting embrace. He trusted her and admired that she'd spent years caring for her brothers.

As he watched her cautiously walk nearer, he couldn't help but think that if he could gaze upon her every day, his world would be a brighter place. Her family was important to her, and he admired that quality. She would make a wonderful mother, and she knew how to run a large household. Not only did that make her a seamless fit into his life, but his clan would welcome her with open arms despite her English heritage.

Jennet floated toward him like a vision his mind might have concocted of the perfect woman. Her gown was dyed a dark, rich indigo and had a scooping neckline that gave a glimpse of alabaster skin. She held up her skirts with their intricately embroidered trim as she moved. Her dress was of the finest quality, and he was certain she was accustomed to having nice possessions.

She might prefer a man with a higher station than a knight, but he had done well for himself and could provide whatever she needed. Even if she had no dowry, he had reliable income from his position with the king and a good home to offer her with his clan.

He blinked, not quite knowing why his thoughts had yet again turned to marriage when he barely knew the lass. There was something genuine about her that made him feel as if the world didn't have to be a treacherous place.

Her gaze darted around the courtyard. After the morning's attack, she might still be wary of the other guests, but she need not fret as long as she was in his presence. He would protect her.

Her worried gaze fell on him, and the strain melted away. Her eyes lit, and he was suddenly standing to greet her as his heart pounded at the anticipation of hearing her lovely voice.

She curtsied. "Good evening, Sir Giric."

"Aye, 'tis now, Lady Jennet." He bowed and reached for her hand, craving the feel of her soft flesh near his own.

She smiled.

"I looked for ye during the meal, but alas, I couldnae find ye."

"After the morning's excitement, my brother was distressed. Then Sybil went missing this afternoon, and he didn't want to let Ada and me out of his sight. So, he arranged for us to take a meal in private."

"Is yer friend unharmed?" Dread spiked in his chest. Should he have sought them out earlier?

"Aye. She returned not long ago." Jennet's relief was plain. "She'd gone out for fresh air because her head was aching, and she said there were too many unfamiliar noises from the hall. She is feeling much better now."

Relief washed over him. He tightened his hand on hers to pull her toward their bench in the shadows. "Are ye enjoying the tourney?"

"Aye. I enjoyed the jousting today. Eddie performed well, and he remained seated." Jennet's smile was genuine.

There was her pride in her family again. He hoped that she would have watched for him if he had chosen to joust.

Every muscle in his body was on edge. She was so near that her leg was flush with his, and her sweet smell invaded all his senses. He wondered if she could sense how lost he was in her.

"Do ye always worry so for yer family?"

"Aye. I admit I do. After the tragedies we've been through, I am a little overprotective."

"I understand. I lost my parents some time ago, and if I could go back to prevent their loss, I would. 'Tis one of the reasons I'm here." He squeezed her hand where it rested on their thighs.

"How would that bring you to England?"

Her curious, direct gaze met his, and for a moment, he

questioned his own judgment. Should he let this lass know that there was a darker side to him…one that couldn't find solace? If he were to pursue her, she had the right to know images and failings from the past still haunted him.

"I'm here to face the man who murdered my father. I seek vengeance." The familiar anger sparked and burned in his chest.

She stilled for a moment, and her gaze focused on their hands before it returned to his.

"Is he here?" Her lips thinned, and where he expected judgment, she squared her shoulders as if she might look after his safety as she did her family's.

"Nae. He has not made an appearance." He swallowed his disappointment. He would still find his revenge. It might just take a little longer than anticipated.

"I am sorry you will not be able to meet him on the field. Perhaps it's a gift from the heavens, and you will now be able to live for what lies before you. I know that in dwelling on the wrongs we cannot change, we sometimes lose what's important now." Her gaze clouded.

He wanted to make the regret in her eyes disappear. Since last night, anytime he'd thought of what lay ahead, his mind had been filled with visions of days and nights of gazing at the woman in front of him. But what if she didn't feel the same?

"What do ye see in yer future?" he asked.

"Freedom." Her chin tilted upward, and he could see the pride and resilience in her magnify. "Since my youth, I've been trapped in one prison or another. But now, I will be allowed to choose my own path."

"And does that road include a husband?" His heart pounded. His interest in her was unexpected, but he sensed that Jennet was the only woman he might ever desire. He craved her as he never had another woman—her ability to make him laugh, her compassion, and her strength of character.

"I wouldn't be adverse should I find someone I believe suitable." She nodded, and even in the dark, her cheeks seemed to grow pinker.

"May I request another favor?"

"You may ask."

His chest tightened. Tilting his body closer to hers, he swallowed, and his free hand lifted to lightly caress her cheek, judging her interest and wondering if he was moving too fast. But everything about this was propitious as if fate had brought them together. The rise and fall of her chest were the only indication she might be experiencing the same desire.

She smiled. "Well, are you going to keep me waiting?" Her teasing tone had returned, but it was huskier, and the sound enveloped him.

"Lady Jennet, may I have a kiss?"

He wanted to do this right, and it wasn't proper to push before she was ready. But anticipation had grabbed him, and his body tensed, both pleasant and terrifying in its intensity.

Her eyes lit, then skirted to the side—he assumed to make certain they weren't being observed. Was she afraid to be seen with him? Had he asked too soon? His breath hitched as he prepared for her denial.

CHAPTER 6

*J*ennet's heart raced as a charged hum vibrated through her. She only barely remembered where they were, and that Ada needed to talk to her brother before she told Eddie that Jennet had found a man she wanted to further her acquaintance with. Giric's place of allegiance didn't matter to her, but Scotland was the one place Eddie and her father had ever forbidden any of their family to return to.

Before, she'd believed all Highlanders were barbarians because no one had tried to save her from her uncle when he'd taken her to his land. Her father's oldest brother had destroyed their lives in his madness, but Giric was different. And although he was seeking recompense for a past wrong, just as her uncle had, she felt her knight would never let his need for revenge come between them.

Yes, this was fast, but nothing had ever felt truer.

Now she knew in her heart that accepting Giric as a suitor and possibly going to Scotland as his wife would free her from the bondage of her past. If she could make new memories in that land with a man who valued her, one she trusted, she would no longer be trapped by the things she couldn't change.

Giric swallowed and stilled as if he were holding his breath. The confident man who had made her laugh and saved her life was suddenly shy and unsure. A flush crept up onto her cheeks.

"Aye, Sir Giric, you have proven yourself worthy of such a favor."

His thumb traced her cheek and sent shivers down her spine. Her core clenched at the prospect of his mouth on hers, and she was having a hard time filling her lungs.

He dipped his head closer and stopped so near that a fresh burst of dark, heady lavender pulled her in and shrouded her in his earthy scent, a smell that was all Giric. One she knew she'd always recognize. He seemed to inhale her as well as his hand slid around her face to clasp the back of her head. His fingers threaded into her hair; sparks flying through her with the intimacy.

He closed the space between them, and his velvety, soft lips landed on hers...sweet, strong, sensual. The embrace was everything, yet her body craved more. It was as if she couldn't get close enough to him. She sighed and tilted farther into the embrace. Time stopped as she let desire and exhilaration absorb her.

When he pulled back, she opened her eyes to his intense scrutiny as fire blazed openly in his stare. He was focused solely on her. A thrill ran through her as she realized his breathing had shallowed as much as her own. Her lips parted, and she brought her fingers to them. A small giggled escaped.

Saints, she was nervous. She never let her emotions run wild, but his touch seemed to knock her senseless.

His fingers caressed her head, and he moved closer yet again. This time when their lips touched, he licked across hers. It surprised her, and she gasped as his tongue darted into her mouth. An inferno erupted inside her, and her breasts tightened.

With each swipe he made, she fell deeper into a spell she'd never been under before. It was like magic, like the sweetest wine, and she knew she would want more. All she desired was for this perfect moment to never end. She clasped his leg to steady herself, but the muscle she felt beneath the fabric was powerful and taut, and she wanted to feel the rest of him.

When he withdrew, his gaze said everything she had been sensing.

Feeling bold, she said, "Sir Giric, you have taken advantage. I granted one kiss." She tilted her head and teased.

"I cannae say I'm sorry, my lady."

She moved closer and whispered, "Your thievery has stolen more than a kiss."

"And what could be more precious than what you freely gave?"

"My senses."

A low rumble came from his chest before the husky burr of his voice filled her ears. "How is that?"

"Is it wrong for me to wish you will do it again?" Just acknowledging it gave her liberty that made her soar like a robin. Other than with her family, and since her father's illness had begun, she'd not felt such security to express her thoughts.

"Nae, 'twould be wrong to deny such a thing."

The curfew bells rang and then a burst of voices pealed from nearby. Remembering they weren't entirely alone, she backed away and instantly missed the heat of his hand on her neck. She glanced up to see a group standing on the opposite side of the gardens. One man ripped a woman from another's arms. He pushed her aside, then attacked the man who had held her. Fists flew, but several other men moved in to pull them apart.

After the confrontation ended, Jennet trembled until Giric's calm arm circled her shoulder and drew her near.

The group moved on, and when they had all cleared the area, her Scottish knight finally spoke. "Yer friends and ye need to be cautious."

"Of what?"

"I didn't find the man from the alley, but when I described him to the local magistrate, the lawman knew of him. He's a paid mercenary."

"That makes no sense. Who would want to harm one of us?"

"I dinnae ken since I couldnae find the arse to question him, but ye need to remain guarded and warn yer friends."

She nodded, and a coolness replaced the warmth of his embrace. She tilted closer toward him, hoping to regain some of the security she felt at having him near.

"And ye should keep yer chamber locked at all times. I'll search for the man again, but if he thinks he might be caught, he might have fled the area."

Her mind was racing. Why would someone want to hurt her or her friends? "I need to tell them straight away."

"I agree. Can I escort ye to yer chamber?"

What if Eddie was there with Ada? She had to approach this sensibly and showing up with a Scottish knight on her arm wouldn't be the best way to win her brother's approval. "No. There are plenty of people about. I'm capable of getting back on my own."

She could see he wanted to protest.

"Let me at least see ye back to the great hall." His eyes pleaded.

She nodded and reluctantly rose, but she still couldn't release her hand from his.

"Will ye be watching the jousts again tomorrow?" he asked as he stood.

"Aye. Will I see you there?"

"I would like that, but 'tis a crowded space. If our paths dinnae cross, will you meet me tomorrow?"

Her heart soared. He'd enjoyed their kisses as much as she.

"Yes. I shall come to this very spot tomorrow at curfew, Sir Giric."

When they parted at the bottom of the stairs, she bounced up to her chamber, already looking forward to seeing him again tomorrow. Upon arriving in their room, it was to find Sybil asleep and Ada missing, perhaps with her brother. She hoped that her friend's words would temper her brother's disdain for all things Scottish.

~

Giric watched Jennet navigate the steps up toward her chamber. He had the urge to follow her to ensure her safety, but if he knew where her room was, he would possibly feel the need to guard her door instead of doing his work for the king or deciphering what kind of man his enemy's son was.

He'd spent most of the afternoon chasing down clues about the attacker's identity instead of doing what he was here for. He wanted to pursue a relationship with the lass, but he couldn't lose any more time with his mission.

But that kiss had knocked him senseless. Perhaps it had been too long since he'd kissed a lass, but he didn't think that was it. There was something special about Jennet. She reached into his soul and made him forget the pain of the past. She made him look forward to the future, something he'd not done since vowing revenge.

Turning, he made his way back into the great hall to pass

through the crowds one more time, and then he retired to his room.

When sleep finally claimed him, his dreams were darkened by images of Edward Linton laughing, then turning his back and walking away, and the solemn girl who had perished all those years ago.

CHAPTER 7

*J*ennet woke with Sir Giric on her mind. Ada hadn't returned to their room, and she was anxious to know if her friend had remembered to talk to her brother. As the sun shone through the window, she sighed and stretched. Ada had told her how she enjoyed sleeping by her brother's side. Jennet wondered what it would be like to wake next to Giric.

He was a large man and would probably take up a good portion of the mattress. But she could imagine waking to have his scent on her and their bedding. Would he hold her as he had when the altercation had happened in the gardens? With his arm around her shoulders, pulling her in, she'd felt a sense of security she'd not known before. Oddly, the closer she was to him, the more she desired to be nearer.

She threw back the covers, ready to start the day and get out of the room. It wasn't that it was stuffy; she just wanted to get out to see if she would happen upon her knight today.

They had been given a large chamber since there were three of them staying in one room. Two beds flanked the window. They also had a fireplace that they hadn't had to use and a small table and chairs where they could take their meal if they wished. Her brother's room was much smaller, so since arriving, their entire group had gathered here instead a few times.

As Jennet's feet hit the floor, Sybil spoke from the second bed. "She didn't return again last night."

"I do think they truly love each other. Let's go out today and see if we can find you someone else to become infatuated with."

Sybil moaned and rose. "It appears you have found someone. Are you sure it's a good idea to give your affections to a man you hardly know?"

"How can you say that? He saved our lives, and besides, we've had some rather involved conversations." She pulled the brush through her hair and tried to remember her friend was having her heart broken right now. Of course she would be a little jealous.

Sybil was fair of face and witty. Today at the jousts, Jennet would make it a point to find someone in attendance who might catch her friend's eye.

"I'm sorry. My head hurts, and I think I shouldn't have skipped the feast last night. Breaking my fast will help my mood." Sybil threw her arms around her in a warm embrace, and Jennet couldn't help but feel there was something bone-deep worrying her friend that she wasn't sharing. Perhaps it was Sybil's brother. She really did need to get out of the man's house and have a little freedom to be herself.

"Sir Giric does appear to be infatuated with you." Sybil pulled back.

"Do you think so?" Her cheeks warmed.

"He gazes upon you as a man who is smitten." They started toward the door.

"Do you have the key? We need to lock the door." Remembering Giric's warning, she scanned the room.

"I'll grab it," Sybil said.

"Sir Giric discovered the man who attacked us was paid

to do so. He said we need to be careful." She shuddered as a fresh chill slid down her spine.

Sybil's face paled, and she froze.

"Don't worry. I think as long as we stick to the crowds and near the castle, we should be safe. He's going to do some more investigating today."

"Did he say what he learned?" Her friend's voice shook.

"Not much, and the man seems to have fled, so I think we probably have nothing more to fear, but even so, be on guard."

They made their way down the stairs for breakfast. Before they were done eating, Ada, Eddie, and Sybil's brother, Lord Roger, had joined them.

As they finished, then rose, Lord Roger spoke. "Lady Jennet, would you please take a walk with me?" And although he'd asked nicely, his hand was already on her arm, guiding her in the direction he wanted.

She cringed inside. "Yes, that would be lovely." She was referring to the fresh air and not the company.

His arms were muscled and stiff, and though he was an attractive man, he was measured and overbearing even when he wasn't ordering people about. Neither spoke as they made their way out of the castle and headed toward the village.

While she'd been eager to catch of glimpse of her knight, she now hoped that he wouldn't see her on Lord Roger's arm. He held onto her as if they were more than acquaintances, which was odd given that he'd only treated her as his sister's friend or a servant in the past.

She'd always felt beneath the earl's notice.

"Are you enjoying the tourney?" She felt the need to break the silence.

"It is affording me the opportunity to make connections that were previously elusive." His reply was formal and calculated.

"Have you met any men whom your sister might form a

connection with?" Perhaps he would help her find a husband, although she wasn't quite sure she trusted the earl's judgment in the matter.

He seemed to stiffen even more, and for the first time, she noticed that though his clothing appeared as impeccable as always, his cheeks had filled in slightly, and a trace of wrinkles creased his brow.

"Ah, yes. There have been a few. I will make a match for her before we leave."

She wanted to ask if he'd let Sybil choose her own husband, but she knew the answer. Everything the earl did was carefully calculated and contrived before he acted. Still, she had to try. "Will Sybil be given a chance to find someone of her liking?"

"Nonsense. Women cannot make these decisions. There are too many things to consider."

Her body tensed, and her heart ached for her friend. She could only hope that whoever the earl chose would be kinder to Sybil than her brother was.

Lord Roger drew her into the bakery, and as she eyed the lemon cakes, he purchased two small plain ones without asking what she liked. He handed one to her as they walked out the door. She wanted to refuse the morsel because her belly was full, but she felt it might offend him, so she picked at it.

She followed his lead as he strolled back toward the castle, thankful that their arms were no longer linked.

"How is your father faring?" Concern colored his tone, and she thought there might be some compassion in his heart.

She supposed now that her father was nearing the end, and Eddie would be taking over, she could be more open. Besides, she was certain Lord Roger had heard the rumors, and he'd been to their estate too many times not to notice something was amiss. Thankfully, some of the times he'd visited were on her father's good days. "He is not well. I'm afraid the healer is saying he will not be with us much longer."

"I'm sorry." He actually sounded sincere.

She nodded, and for the first time since arriving, she let her father's state consume her. They'd had a long time to deal with his debilitation, but over the last month, he'd been more withdrawn and had begun sleeping most of the day away. The healer had said that he would probably last the month, that they had time to attend the tourney and return before he would pass.

"I will seek out your brother today. I believe it's time you are wed, and I am in need of a wife." She froze as he continued on. He stopped, and his scrutiny narrowed on her.

She must have heard him wrong. Her chest felt like the time she'd fallen from a tree and onto her back. She couldn't breathe. Lord Roger gave her a brief, tight smile, then tugged her along.

No, no, no. Why would he even think they suited? Her heart stilled, and her belly churned. She didn't want to offend him, but he was one of the last men she would choose.

Taking a deep breath, she composed herself before speaking. She had to let him know his pursuit was foolish, and she wasn't interested. "I am being wooed by another, Lord Roger. I'm afraid he has quite stolen my heart."

"Who is this other man?" He took her arm and led her toward the castle.

"He is a knight." She was reluctant to give his name. They'd not made any formal declaration, though, despite the short time, she was confident he would offer for her.

"Has he compromised you?" There was an edge to his tone.

Her mouth fell open, and she found no words would pass her lips.

"Has he taken you to his bed?" he barked.

She snapped her mouth shut, then finding her voice, she drew her shoulders back and stood taller. "No. He is a man of honor."

Lord Roger seemed to relax, but a ruthless gleam ignited in his eyes as if he were planning some move on a chess-board, cold and calculating.

He didn't speak, so she continued. "There are many eligible ladies here. I can help find someone who would be a more fitting match for you."

His grip on her arm tightened. "Nonsense. We will address this when I speak with Edward."

Her only solace was that her family had made a vow that they would all marry for love. Eddie would support her. Yet despite her confidence, a cold premonition spread down her spine and settled in her bones. She knew Eddie looked up to the earl, and Lord Roger was a man accustomed to being obeyed.

However, in this matter, he would not prevail.

The walk back to the castle was painfully awkward, with Lord Roger's steely grip not releasing her until they were standing outside her door. It was unlocked, and he pushed his way in, towing her behind him. His gaze fell on her, icy and conniving. She shivered. And for a moment, fear seared her insides. Had he planned to get her alone and take advantage so that he could force her into a match?

"How was your walk?"

He froze when Ada's voice came from farther in the chamber. She was standing at the dressing table.

"It's a lovely day," Jennet hedged, not wanting to express her concerns in front of Lord Roger.

"Where is Edward?" His question sliced through the air, and concern spread through her as she realized he was not taking her rejection well.

"He is with his squire, preparing to attend the jousts today."

Roger finally let go of her arm. "Tell my sister to come see me when she returns," he ordered, then turned and left the room without another word.

"What was that about? He's usually stiff, but he seemed cross." Ada's mouth twisted with disgust.

"I'll tell you later." She wanted to wipe Lord Roger's demands from her memory. She needed to know she would still have her freedom. "First, I have to know, did you talk to Eddie?"

"Yes, he said that of course, your husband is your choice."

She let air fill her lungs, then gave a gleeful sigh. Relief that Ada had talked to Edward before Roger could overwhelmed her, and she barely restrained an urge to bounce up and down.

"He just wants to meet Sir Giric. He said he'd not hand his sister over to a Scot without judging the man's merits first, but that he mostly trusted your judgment." Ada laughed.

Ah, thank heavens. Now all she had to do was find her knight and make the introduction. Eddie would probably be as enamored with Sir Giric as she was.

~

Giric stood near a merchant's tent that was set near the outskirts of the jousting field and kept his gaze glued to the two men arguing nearby. It appeared Edward Linton had made some enemies of his own, and this one was a powerful adversary—the Earl of Bruton. Giric recognized him as the man who had joined Edward yesterday morning in the village.

He moved closer, pretending to look at the wares as he listened to the heated words between the men.

"We have been friends for a long time. Do not ask this of me." Edward Linton shook his head.

"There is no one better suited to the position." The earl stood tall and glared down at Edward as if scolding him.

"No. It's my father's will, and I'll not dispute him." At the mention of his enemy, Giric's hand clenched on the handle of the knife he was pretending to inspect.

"If your father was thinking clearly, he would change his mind," the earl said.

Edward took a deep breath. "Roger, I would do almost anything for you, but this is not my choice."

"Aye. You have every say." The earl's voice rose.

"My answer is no. I have been told she has already chosen." Edward stood his ground, drawing his shoulders back and staring straight into the earl's eyes.

"Then it will come to this. I challenge you on the jousting field."

Giric heard Edward's sharp intake of air. "Then I have no recourse but to accept."

"You will soon find out that no one defies me." The earl marched off, leaving Edward looking bewildered and lost.

Giric almost felt a pang of empathy for the man. He seemed to be torn between loyalties.

Setting down the knife and turning, he followed Edward's movements as the man made his way toward the jousting field, but he didn't stop there, instead heading toward the camp. Possibly to instruct his squire to ready his jousting equipment.

Giric didn't follow for fear of being too obvious in his study. Besides, he had things to ponder on.

This was an unfortunate turn of events. What if the earl hurt the baron's son before Giric could face him on the battlefield? He had no control of the joust, and their rivalry could damage his chances of getting to his true enemy. He would keep a close watch on both the men.

As he came up next to the viewing box, he saw her, the woman who had consumed his thoughts almost as much as his quest. Jennet was watching knights as they rode across the field, then turning and making comments to her friends. Her smile was warm and genuine, and he longed to taste her lips again. He was tempted to go to her now, but he tamped down the urge to take her hand. He had work to do.

To avoid temptation, he made his way to the opposite end of the stands, to a position where he could see the jousts but also put the temptation from his mind.

What felt like hours later, he watched as the Earl of Bruton and Edward Linton took the field. As they trotted past each other on the first pass, it was Edward who made a solid strike and broke his lance. The crowd cheered loudly.

It appeared to be a fairly even match, except that the earl had a scheming deliberation to his movements that chilled Giric's bones. He'd seen men similar to him on the battle-field, ones who were in control of every situation, ones who seemed void of feelings inside.

On the second attempt, both men hit their marks and broke their lances. The blow was deafening, and the roar from the gathered crowd rang in his ears. Edward teetered in his saddle and was almost unseated when the earl's lance slid down Edward's armor and almost caught at his knee.

Giric shook his head. Although the blow was within regulations, he could tell the earl had purposely gone for Edward's injured leg. He wanted to see all the Lintons account for the death of his father, but he would do it honor-ably. Bruton had no integrity.

The earl earned the point.

The third pass was the same, and this time when the earl's lance caught Edward square then slid down toward his injured leg, he fell from his steed and landed with a thud. For a moment, fear, anger, and despair mixed together as Giric thought his chance for revenge might be gone, stolen at the hands of a pompous earl.

Men rushed out to help Edward to his feet, and he stood

then bowed to the stands to indicate he was uninjured, but his limp was a little more pronounced as he left the field.

The Earl of Bruton was declared the winner.

Edward's visor was removed. The earl strode up to him, and although Giric couldn't hear the words that were exchanged, he could see the heat, then the defeat on his enemy's son's face. Edward shook his head, and then both men glanced at the stands.

Giric's thoughts turned to what Edward's challenger would demand as reward for his win. As long as he was able to meet Edward on the field during the melee, it wouldn't matter.

CHAPTER 8

*J*ennet paced the chamber as the afternoon sun burst through the windows. The room was sticky and stale. Home at Cresthaven, this type of heat usually signaled a coming storm. She wanted to run back down to the camp where Eddie's squire was probably helping him remove his armor, but she knew there was nothing she could do for him when he was amongst the men. Her brother would not want to show any weakness in front of them, so she'd gathered a distraught Ada and Sybil, and come here to wait for Eddie to return.

Her insides were still frozen from reliving the horror of her brother's last fall from a horse and how long his recovery had taken. Why had he made such a foolish decision? She should have insisted that he not participate in these dangerous pursuits. But would he have listened? He was a grown man now, and she was not his mother.

The door swung in. Eddie stood in the doorway with what looked like a forced grin upon his face. If he was trying to convince them that he was unharmed, she wasn't fooled.

"Are you injured?" Ada rushed to Eddie's side as soon as he hobbled into the room.

He only shook his head as he limped across the small space and eased into a seat at the table. Pain was etched on his face in tight lines even as he smiled and tried to hide his suffering.

"I'm whole. It's mostly my pride that's taken the beating."

Ada touched his cheek. "Here, take this." She handed him her wine, and he took a couple of large gulps, then set the goblet on the table before pulling her in for a hug. And not for the first time, Jennet said a prayer of thanks that Eddie had her friend, who would love and care for him for the rest of their lives. She would be the best medicine for him.

When Ada backed away, Eddie was silent a moment, then he shook his head, likely still upset with his loss today. Jennet didn't care about whether or not he'd won, just that he was unharmed.

His eyes met Jennet's then darted away before he grumbled something inaudible and reached for the glass of wine. At the same time, Sybil reached for the platter of cheese and meats. She misjudged the distance and knocked into the tray, which hit the glass and spilled the red liquid.

"Oh, I'm so sorry. I'll clean it up and get you another." Sybil picked up a cup to replace the toppled one, filled it, and handed it to him.

"How's your leg?" Jennet asked.

"Not too bad. It will just be sore for a few days."

"What were you thinking? You know Roger's reputation." She wanted to shake Eddie for being so careless. He could have been truly hurt again.

He gave her a defeated look. She'd not seen him so distraught since the day they'd realized their father's wits were gone. Something awful was bothering him, and it wasn't his old injury or a new one. This went beyond physical.

Her stomach flipped, and suddenly, she wished she'd

skipped the snack that Sybil had ordered for their room. Had Roger taken her refusal to marry him out on Edward?

"I need to speak with you alone." His sad gaze shifted from her to the floor, and his shoulders seemed to pull in on themselves. Worry assailed her.

"What is it?"

He shook his head, and then his regard traveled to Ada and Sybil. What could he not say in front of them? They shared almost everything. Was there word from home? Had the healer been wrong about how much time their father had? Her eyes stung.

Ada swayed and grabbed the back of Eddie's chair. She shook her head. "Edward," came from her lips, but the words were muted in an uncharacteristically soft tone.

He glanced up to see Ada blink a couple times, then stagger. "Edward," she repeated.

"Are you all right?" Sybil was the first one to react, rushing in and clinging to Ada's side to steady her.

Ada leaned against Sybil as Eddie rose and took her other side. "I don't feel well. I think it's all the excitement."

"Let's get her to the bed." Sybil took charge. "I think she needs to rest."

Jennet rushed to pull the covers back as the pair guided her toward the bed. As they lay her down, Ada continued, "I think I just need some rest." She closed her eyes, and only a few minutes later was in a fitful, dream-filled sleep.

They took turns pacing around the room until Eddie said, "I'll keep watch on her. Why don't you two get some fresh air?"

"Aye. We should let her rest." Jennet wrung her hands. Last time she'd seen someone this ill so suddenly, it had been her mother just before she gave birth to William and then left the world.

"Come, Jennet. Let's take a stroll." Sybil took her arm.

She didn't want to leave Ada, but she knew no one would

take better care of her than Eddie. She nodded. Whatever he had wanted to tell her would have to wait until Ada was better.

As they left the castle, Sybil said, "I wonder what was going on between Roger and Edward."

"I think I know. Your brother asked for my hand earlier today."

A sharp intake of air indicated that her friend had not known of her brother's plans. Sybil closed her eyes, let out a slow breath, and looked down at her hands as they twisted around her chatelaine.

"I told him no, and he was probably seeking retribution for my denial." Jennet shook her head. She should have handled it differently. The last thing they needed was a rivalry with Roger. As their close neighbor, he'd been a friend to Eddie for years, almost serving more like a father than their real one, who hadn't been mentally present for most of Eddie's formidable years. Guilt stabbed at her as she realized she might have caused irreparable damage to their bond.

"You can't wed him. You know how he is. You'll be trapped like me." Sybil's tone took on a panicked quality, which did nothing to allay her own fears.

"I'm aware. He's most likely angry by my refusal. I told him I'd given my heart to another."

"Sir Giric?"

"Aye, and I know it's been a short time, but he is the one. We have this connection that I've never had with another man. It sounds fanciful, but I think fate has brought us together."

"Then you were correct to deny my brother, and you should see if this knight harbors the same feelings for you."

She was about to agree when Sybil continued, "Ah, what luck. There is your knight right there."

She turned to look in the direction Sybil was pointing.

Her pulse increased at the sight of Giric, laughing with some other knights near the edge of the viewing stands. Her heart leapt, and she couldn't contain the smile that bubbled up.

"Go to him. I'll be fine. I'll seek out my brother and find out what he's thinking." Sybil patted her shoulder.

"You are certain you want to face him right now?"

"Aye. It's probably the best time since he'll be high from his victory."

"Be careful." She nodded.

"Aye. I will. Enjoy your time with your knight. Perhaps he will ask you to wed him before the evening is over."

Sybil embraced her, then pivoted and darted back toward the castle. Jennet watched her go. A tremor ran down her spine, and she worried for a moment that Roger might decide to take his anger out on his sister. Sybil had always given in to his orders, but lately she'd begun standing up to him, and Jennet wasn't sure how long her friend would be able to stay under his roof without dire repercussions.

She had to get Sybil away from Roger. Perhaps one of the men Giric was with would be looking for a wife. Swiveling toward the fields, she noticed the men had broken from their group, and Giric had spotted her. He glided toward her like a boat set on its course.

She was rooted to the spot, watching as he strode straight for her as if they already belonged to one another. Her heart thumped loudly. And there was no doubt in her mind that after only a couple days, she knew he was the man for her. She felt free with him, and she hadn't experienced that since she was a young child. She had prayed for her freedom, for a man who would let her be who she was, and she'd found him.

Joy sparked in her chest. She checked to be certain her hair was in place, then started toward her knight.

When he was standing in front of her, the only word that came out was, "Hello."

"Good day, my lady." The possessive shimmer in his tone wrapped around her and eased the worries of the afternoon.

"Have you been watching the jousts?"

"Aye. They've been competitive today. A lot of men have been unseated. I believe the healers will be busy this afternoon."

She thought to tell Giric about Eddie's injury, but she didn't want to talk about her brother, so she didn't mention him. She didn't want to think about anything sad. She was with her knight, and all she desired was to feel his arms around her. "Are you off to somewhere, or can you take a lady for a stroll? I am without a companion."

"And why does a lovely lass find herself alone?"

"My brother is caring for Ada, who has fallen ill, and Sybil has business to see to."

"I am sorry yer friend is no' feeling well."

She nodded. "You see then, I find myself in a predicament. I'm in need of the company of an honorable knight to keep me from idly wandering about and finding mischief."

"Aye, Lady Jennet. I can think of no other lass I would wish to guard more. 'Tis my good fortune to find ye in need of a companion."

"You truly are a chivalrous knight."

"Do ye mind if I take the lead? There is a place I have found that I'd like to share with ye." He drew her hand to his and guided her farther from the castle. The familiar spark of recognition teased her when his calloused fingers twined with hers.

"Have you earned enough trust for a lone lady to follow you wherever you may lead?" She giggled, her worries fading to the back of her mind as she vowed to relish her coming freedom and the thrill of spending the rest of the afternoon with Giric.

"If I havenae done so, I intend to try."

"I think you have tempted me to test fate yet again." She enjoyed their banter.

Was she being too bold? How was it she felt as if she'd known this man all her life? It was as though neither of them had been completely whole until just two nights past. She couldn't help thinking that after years of living for others, life had finally given her reason for being.

"Yer faith honors me. And perhaps ye can finish the tale of what happened with yer family."

"Aye. I'd enjoy that. I haven't spoken of it in years, and I find releasing the words might be freeing." It was refreshing to be comfortable expressing her thoughts with him.

"Well, I will hold ye if 'twill help." A wide grin spread across his full lips.

Was he jesting? She wasn't quite sure. She thought he might be, but a shiver of anticipation slid down her neck, and she thought she would like it if he did so.

"Where was I?" She sighed and attempted to remember where she'd left off. "Ah, when my uncle realized that my mother had chosen my father instead of him. He attacked my father and nearly killed him. My grandfather was so incensed that he disinherited my uncle."

"'Tis tragic." His eyes held truth and understanding.

Longing reached in and twirled binds around her heart, slowly tying her soul to his.

"That was not the end of it. My uncle disappeared for six years." Her mind took her back to that time, and a shudder snaked through her limbs before a numbness washed over her. She inched closer to Giric as they entered a well-trodden path that led into the dense forest beyond the camp.

"Did they make amends when he returned?"

"No. He'd spent years plotting his retribution. He came to steal away my mother." The shock on Giric's face mirrored the tremor that still racked her when she thought of her uncle.

His grip tightened on her hand. The gesture was comforting. "Was he successful?"

"No, my mother had passed a year earlier, giving birth to my youngest brother, William." She shuddered at the memory.

"Och, I ken what 'tis like to lose a parent. What did yer uncle do?"

"He still hated my father and was intent on his revenge. He seized on an easy mark. My maid had been out with me in a field near the castle. I'd been practicing with my bow, and on the way home, we stopped to pick red clover to make flower crowns."

She swallowed the lump that lodged in her throat, then continued, "He took me in her stead."

Giric stopped, and his fingers stiffened in her grip. "How could he? Ye were but a child?"

"Aye. I was only seven summers. He hid me away in a place he thought my family would never find." She gave Giric a tight smile, then nodded that they could continue along the path.

"But yer father found ye?"

"He did, but it took five years." She said it flippantly, but those years had been terrifying and endless. Knowing no one and being restricted as a prisoner, she still had night tremors over the ordeal.

"What did yer uncle do to ye?" Hesitation and anger colored Giric's voice.

"He treated me like I was mud on his boots. He kept me locked away and forced me to clean and cook. He was so worried about my father's wrath that he wouldn't let me leave his home. If others were about, he forced me to pretend that he was my sire."

"But yer father found ye?" Giric repeated, his hand tightening on hers.

"I was twelve when my family came for me." They

reached a gurgling, fast-flowing brook. Large stones lay on the bank, a couple wide enough to sit on comfortably. Giric eased onto one and drew her near him.

She was quiet for a moment. She swallowed past the constriction in her throat. "But although they found me that day, we lost much more."

Giric remained silent as if he were trying to wrap his mind around her words.

She shook her head and took a deep breath. He seemed to understand that she'd given more of herself than she normally did. She couldn't say any more, and he didn't push, but her thoughts turned to her eldest brother, Richard, and how he'd rushed in to save her as her father and uncle fought, and then how he'd gone back in to save her father once the fire had started.

Her father had made it out, but he'd been badly burned. Richard had perished in the blaze that day. They'd left Scotland a broken shell of a family, and her father was never the same. He'd saved one child, only to lose another.

Instead of dwelling on her family's loss, she changed the subject. "This is a lovely spot. How did you find it?"

"I went exploring yesterday. With so many people about, I desired a place to be where I could have peace. It made me think of ye."

"I'm happy you brought me to see it." It was just what she'd needed this afternoon.

He nodded and glanced over the water as they held hands. She leaned her shoulder into his and enjoyed the feel of his strong, solid frame. "Tell me about your home," she said.

He inhaled and gripped her hand a little tighter, and she knew he was about to confide in her as she had in him.

~

What could Giric say? That he'd not felt at home anywhere until he'd met her? That seemed crazy. Although he'd only known her a few days, Jennet was the right woman for him. But did she feel the same? The slant of her body into his said she might.

"My mother was the younger sister to the queen consort of Scotland. She died from an illness when I was very young. My father was The MacDonald, Lord of the Isles. I have two older brothers, one of whom was just entering adulthood when he became the leader of the clan."

"From what I've heard of clans, that is a huge responsibility." She nodded in understanding.

"Aye, and my aunt thought it was too much for him to take on and to have to worry with me at the same time."

"What did you do?" she asked.

He wondered if she knew she was thrumming her thumb across his in encouragement. He liked that she did it naturally, without thinking about what she was doing.

"She brought me to court to train with the king's men and be her ward until my brother was well established."

"And have you been back?"

"My home is on the Isle of Skye, but my place recently has been at my king's side. 'Tis been too long."

"Do you wish to return to Skye?"

"Aye, more than anything. I am pleased to serve with my king, but my heart will always be with my clan."

She sat up and met his eyes directly. "You have earned another point, Sir Giric. A man who puts family above all else is someone to be valued." Her tone was teasing, but he knew she meant it.

"Have ye ever been to Scotland?"

"Aye. It is where my uncle hid me away." Her lips thinned.

"Well, if ye allow, I'll take ye there, and ye can make memories that are pleasing." His heart beat faster. Thinking of Jennet as his wife and being back with the clan was a desire he'd not truly acknowledged until now.

"And, Sir Giric, what boon do you think ye have won that I would accompany ye to such a place?"

"If ye see the Highlands the way I do, 'twill be enough of a reward in the viewing."

"How does it compare to this?" She held out her free hand to encompass the beauty of the stream and forest before them.

"Ah, this cannae compare. Ye have to see the rich green mountains for yerself. Most have streams of water falling from their peaks and cliffs."

"Perhaps one day I will see it."

"'Twill be the most beautiful thing ye've ever laid yer eyes upon. There is only one thing that could make it bonnier."

"What would that be?"

"Ye." He reached out, touched her cheek with the back of his hand, and pulled it slowly and tenderly up the smooth surface. Yearning spread through him. He inched closer, his thigh so near hers that longing extended out from the point and tunneled its way through every part of him.

His gaze was drawn to her full, wine-colored lips, and the temptation to kiss her surged in his blood. He met her eyes and saw his own need reflected in their brown depths. Jennet's mouth fell open, an invitation he would not let pass.

Instead of diving in, he drew her into his lap, and she slid her arm around his waist. The soft weight of her was like a soothing blanket, except instead of calming, her nearness excited him more. When seated on him, her face was level with his.

As he savored the feel of her, she leaned in and placed her mouth on his, sending a rush of need into him. She couldn't know what she was doing to him with the simple, innocent kiss. He tightened his grip on her as he deepened the embrace.

She tasted like honey, desire, and temptation. He was swept away on a tide of feelings that were new to him. He'd kissed other ladies, but none that had made his chest pulse as if it would implode if he were to let her go.

She moved, exploring his mouth with a slow curiosity that drew out the delicious torturous hunger pulsing in his veins. She shifted, the pressure from her rear rubbing against his sensitive cock. He groaned into her mouth.

Och, he wanted to do more than kiss her. His thoughts strayed into an unchivalrous vision of him pulling up her skirts and impaling her with his hard staff, letting her wiggle on him slowly and drawing out the sweet pain until his seed filled her and made her his. His body had never reacted so to another.

Her hand curled on his shoulder, firm, solid, and intimate. He couldn't tell if she was indicating the embrace was too much or that she felt the same uncontrollable burn that had lit deep inside his core. He'd almost tuned out the rest of the world, but somewhere in the back of his consciousness, he was aware that others knew of this place, and just a little farther upstream, the men and women from the camp had set up an area for bathing. Although he would never take her for the first time here, just being seen kissing her could force her into a marriage she might not want. He had to be sure she would wed him, and he needed to seek out her brother, before they took this to its conclusion.

Family was important to her, and he knew she would want her brother's blessing before they wed.

He reluctantly pulled back, breathless, shocked, and fighting the loss of his control.

"Did I do something wrong?" Her eyes filled with worry, but her chest still rose and fell as she struggled for breath. Her lips appeared fuller, and her chin was red from where her soft skin had rubbed against his jaw.

He loved the thoroughly kissed look on her.

"Nae, lass." He decided to continue being honest with her. "Ye have awoken a part of me that wants to do more than just taste yer sweet mouth."

She blushed as a broad smile spread across her face.

"And I feel as if I should seek out yer brother before we take this beyond a place he would approve of."

"You are the most honorable of knights. I commend your resolve, but what if I am a lady who desires to discover what you could be eluding to?" She teased, but her boldness was tempered with a blush.

His chest rumbled. "Soon. I promise that when I do show ye, it will be in a time and place where we can draw out the pleasure for both of us. As lovely as this spot is, too many camp followers frequent the water here, and it is not the right location for that lesson."

Standing, he let himself relish her nearness for just a moment longer before she slid down his body as he set her gently on her feet.

"I will take you to meet my brother tonight. I think you and Eddie will come to like each other quite easily."

Taking her hand, he guided her back toward the path and a place where he wouldn't be tempted to give in to the fire still pulsing through his veins. He would ask her brother's permission if they could wed. When she was his, he could take his time showing her everything.

A strange thought hit him—he didn't yet know her family name.

He would discover it soon enough when she made the introduction tonight. But for now, it didn't matter who her family was. She was going to be his.

CHAPTER 9

*J*ennet's legs were still wavering and unsteady. How had a kiss shaken her down to her core, made her forget all her reserve, and called on her to beg him for another? She'd been brazen, and that was so unlike her, but she loved the freedom that sang in her blood when she was near Giric. Her mother had died when she was young, and all she had were brothers, no one to teach her what to expect when a man and woman were courting. Only what she'd heard from Ada, but she'd pushed that information away because the last thing she wanted to hear about was her best friend and her brother's private time.

Giric had been tender. She'd been so caught up in the feel of him that she wasn't sure she would have stopped his advances had he tried to take her. He was an honorable man, and despite her lack of knowledge, she was confident he would be a patient and attentive teacher. Moisture pooled at the juncture of her legs as she thought about her skin touching his in intimate places.

By the time they returned to the castle, the sun was dipping low in the sky.

"Shall we find something to fill our bellies before we seek out yer brother?" he asked.

"Aye. I think we shall."

They sat at a bench among the other guests in the great hall, but they barely spoke to anyone else. They laughed and talked about goals and dreams and silly things like stories of the fae and cold baths. They discussed serious matters such as the absence of King Richard and the strife between England and Scotland. They conversed as if they'd known each other their entire lives. Their connection was real and tangible, and this was what she wanted every day from a partner.

Hours passed before she realized how late it was. The curfew bells had long ago rung, and most of the guests had already left the feast, seeking their beds for the evening.

As they walked up the stairs toward her room, it wasn't trepidation she felt, but anticipation at introducing Eddie to the man she would like to choose for a husband. She'd hoped to see her brother at dinner, but when he'd not made an appearance, she thought he might still be watching over Ada.

Reaching the door, she knocked gently, hoping not to wake her friend if she were still resting.

Sybil opened the door, nodded at her and Giric, then squeezed out into the hall.

"How is she?" Jennet whispered.

"Not much better. Your brother has fallen ill as well, although he doesn't seem as bad. They're both sleeping."

Worry gripped her. Eddie never got sick. It was years of mothering him, their younger brother, and father that had her reaching for the knob again.

Sybil placed her hand on Jennet's, looked at Giric, then back at her. "I wouldn't go in there if I didn't have to. There is an odor."

"Oh, no," she said.

"I'll tend to them tonight, and you can tomorrow. You should stay with Sir Giric."

"I don't think that is wise," she countered.

Leaning in, Sybil whispered into her ear, "Roger is coming by in a little while. He's quite cross, and you probably don't want to see him."

He must be behaving as a tyrant if Sybil was warning her away. Jennet shuddered to think about what Roger might do if he came by and found Giric here after her dismissal today.

Her friend backed away, and before she could reply, Sybil continued out loud, "Your brother would want to make sure you stay healthy. We shall take turns, so we can rest. He won't mind."

Ada must have told Sybil that Eddie was going to let her choose Sir Giric.

"Are you certain?" Taking a deep breath, she thought over the consequences. She was going to marry Giric anyway. She was certain he was going to ask. And she'd had such an amazing time with him this afternoon. Why not stay with him? He was honorable, and she knew nothing would take place that she didn't want to happen.

She glanced back at Giric. Heart pounding, she asked, "Can I stay with you tonight?"

His mouth fell open. Then he shut it. He swallowed. His gaze traveled to the door, and his lips thinned ever so slightly. His conscience must be getting to him. What was a worthy knight to do in such a situation? Honestly, either choice was understandable, but time seemed to freeze, and her breath caught. What if he said no? Had she misread all his signals? Her belly began to twist.

"Aye. I can sleep on the floor."

Relief flooded her. But there was no way she was going to let him sleep on the ground. Now the prospect of being in his room excited her. She wasn't worried about sneaking into his chamber. There were a handful of people here at the tourney who knew her, and chances of any of them seeing her were slim.

She focused on Sybil. "I will be back at daybreak. That way, you can rest, and I'll watch over them."

Sybil nodded.

"Oh, wait." She thought for a moment. "If you need my help during the night, come find me."

Turning to Giric, she asked, "Can you tell Sybil how to find your room?"

"Aye." He pointed toward the stairs. "Up one flight, then my chamber is the sixth door on the left."

"And I'll tie a kerchief on the handle just to make sure you can find it." Jennet hoped Eddie and Ada would improve during the night, but this made her feel a little better about leaving them.

"I'll take good care of them." Sybil was reassuring and sincere as she gave a tight smile.

"Just be certain to come find me if you require any assistance. Thank you." She hugged Sybil, then she and Giric turned and walked toward the steps.

As they entered his room, she breathed in the scent that clung to the small space. Male and musk, all Giric. When he bolted the door, she turned to take him in. An illicit thrill filled her, and although Sybil might be overreacting to Lord Roger's rage, she was glad her friend had pushed her in this direction.

What else could she learn about Giric? And was now the time to ask the question that had been burning in her brain? Perhaps tonight she could broach the one reservation she had about her Scottish knight.

～

J ennet looked lovely standing in his chamber. Giric's palms itched to touch her, to caress her curves and make her his. But he couldn't do that yet.

His eyes darted around, looking for the best place to prepare a pallet on the floor. He took the extra blanket from the bed and walked over to an empty space.

"No. You won't be sleeping on the floor."

His gaze drifted toward the bed, and he was certain the color must have drained from his face.

"I believe you to be honorable, and I will not sleep thinking of you on the cold, hard timber. The bed is large enough for us both to have room."

His mouth was dry, and he couldn't think of what to say. All he could focus on was that Jennet was going to be in his bed tonight.

"Do you have a spare tunic?" she asked.

"Aye, I do." He nodded and swallowed…hard.

"May I use it?"

"Aye." He grabbed one from his trunk and handed it to her. "I'll turn."

As he fought the urge to peek over his shoulder, his thoughts strayed to what he would wear. He typically slept without clothing, but she'd learn that once they were wed. His groin tightened. He would have to wear a short tunic as well, but still, they would be so close.

Moonlight filtered in through the window, providing enough light to move around, so he didn't bother with a candle. Only moments later, they had both changed, and as they climbed beneath the covers, she let out a contented sigh. The glow was comforting and gave an air of magic to the night. He lay there, letting the world outside the walls disappear, knowing when he woke in the morning, he'd have to seek out her brother straight away. He wanted to forget how lonely he'd felt the last few years and start anew with the woman who made him smile, laugh, and desire.

Although he was prone on his back, staring at the timbers of the ceiling, he could feel the warmth from her presence. His body hummed. He wanted to draw her into his arms and revel in the feel of her, but knowing if he did and if she were willing, their embrace might proceed into an intimacy he couldn't allow just yet. He twined his fingers together on his belly. His cock ached at the inevitability of their joining.

The mattress beneath him shifted, and he glanced her way to discover that she studied him in the dim illumination of the chamber. Then her palm rested on his chest, and his pulse spiked. Her touch set his already heated body ablaze.

"Giric."

"Aye, lass." The strain in his body was reflected in a throaty reply.

"Tell me about the revenge you seek." The hint of fear and disapproval in her voice was like cold seawater splashing him. Would she try to persuade him to abandon his plan?

"There isnae much to say. The baron killed my father, and I seek retribution." She didn't flinch at his words, but she seemed to still.

"What happened?" Her hand remained on his chest.

Confident he'd not yet scared her away, he continued, "My father and I were visiting cousins to the south. While there, I was delivering a message to a man about buying one of his horses. I found the man mistreating a child. I told my father, and he bade me to stay with our cousin as he sought an audience with the arse."

"That's awful." She snuggled closer.

"When he didn't come back, we went there and discovered that my father, the tavern owner, and the child had all been murdered. It took days of questioning the nearby villagers to discover the identity of the English nobleman who had fled from the area."

"I'm so sorry. You know that's not your fault?" One of her fingers made circles, searing him through his tunic.

"It feels as if I had stayed out of it, my father would be here today."

"You can't know that."

No, he couldn't, but he was certain things would have been different if he'd not gotten involved. He remained silent.

"Will you kill the man?"

"I planned to challenge him, but he isnae here."

"Then you won't need to fight." Relief sounded in her voice.

"Nae, I have waited too long, and my father's honor demands justice. I will challenge his son to a fair battle during the melee."

"And if you best him and he yields, will you kill him?" Her fingers trembled on his chest.

"Nae. But I will demand the life of his father."

She gasped, but he wouldn't hide the truth from her. She deserved to know who he truly was.

"And then will you be satisfied?"

"I want the baron's family to suffer as mine has." He couldn't keep the raw anger from his tone, and his words were harsh.

"What if he bests you?" she asked.

"Then, I will be defeated, knowing that I sought justice for my family."

"Do your brothers feel the same way you do?"

"No. They weren't there when it happened. They don't…" He swallowed hard and admitted the truth he'd not said to anyone else. "…Blame themselves."

Her hand stroked his chest. It was meant to be a soothing motion, and she likely did it without thinking. He would bet that she didn't even realize she was comforting him with her touch, but the sweet gesture meant everything to him.

"You are not to blame, and your father wouldn't wish that burden for you. He would probably want you to live for the present and not dwell on what you cannot change."

He clasped her hand, pulled it to his lips, and placed his mouth on her sweet flesh. He kissed her on her knuckles because he was afraid if he did it the proper way, he'd want too much. He didn't believe her words, but it was endearing that she had so much faith in him after knowing him for such a short time.

"That is kind of ye. But after this tournament, I can have peace and move on." *Hopefully, with ye.*

"I do wish for you to find solace. Vengeance rarely leads down the path you desire."

She was correct, but justice had been his mission for years, and he would not dishonor his father by failing to see it through, even for the woman he wanted by his side.

He placed her palm back on his chest. It was the one touch that he would allow himself tonight. "Rest. It sounds as if ye will have a busy day caring for yer brother and friend tomorrow."

And he had to spend a little more time with their host. Meeting Jennet's brother might have to wait until he was hale and hearty. Knowing she'd be caring for them tomorrow, he could focus on his other task.

CHAPTER 10

*A*s the chamber brightened with a warm, new-day glow, Jennet stretched then angled onto her side to look at the braw knight who lay peacefully next to her. She didn't like that he had his mind set on righting wrongs that hadn't been within his control, but she did like everything else about him—his strong chin, the trust he'd shown in her last night by not shielding her from his truth, and the way his lips curled when he smiled.

She'd tasted those lips. And she wanted to again.

He'd turned to face her during the wee hours of the morning, and now she was astonished by the comfort she felt at being so near him. It was as if they'd known each other for years instead of mere days. Trailing her fingers down his well-muscled arm, she reveled in the heat that seeped through his tunic, tempting her to scoot closer and nestle near to him. His heavy lids opened. They were hooded and sensual and seemed to plead with her to take another kiss. But he spoke before she had a chance to act on the urge.

"Ye are a bonny sight to wake to." His morning voice was husky, and it rolled over her like the warmth she felt when walking into Cresthaven's kitchens on a cold winter night.

"I was thinking the same thing."

"'Tis still early. I think we can get ye back to yer room before the castle wakes." He threw back the covers, and a rush of cool air *whooshed* over her. She rather thought she wanted to stay here, next to Giric, but he seemed eager to have her gone. It was unexpected and stung just a little bit. She'd been but seconds away from claiming his mouth.

Her hurt feelings must have shown on her face because he continued, "I would like to linger, but we have to see to yer honor."

It was a valid reason for rushing her out the door, and she had to remember that his need to be in the right was one of the qualities she admired most about him.

"Very well." She did need to see to Ada and Eddie. She rose and strolled over to the chair where she'd placed her gown last evening.

He turned to face the other direction as he dressed, allotting her privacy as she did the same for him. When they were ready, he escorted her down to her room.

He took both her hands in his. "Will I see ye this evening?"

"Aye. At our bench, and if Eddie is well, I'll bring you back up to meet him."

"I will count the moments until I see ye again." His gaze was sincere.

Her heart skipped a beat at his declaration. She didn't want to part, but they both had duties to attend. "I will, as well."

She expected him to close the distance between them and kiss her again, but instead, he drew her hands to his lips and caressed her flesh. Rising, he said, "Until tonight," then dropped her hands and turned to walk away.

She sighed, standing still with her hand on the knob as she followed his movements until he was out of view. Then she turned to open the door. As she slid in easily and quietly, she scolded herself for not reminding her friends to bolt the door. They shouldn't be so careless since there still might be a mercenary attempting to hunt one of them down.

Ada and Eddie were sleeping on one bed, while Sybil was spread out on the other. All rested peacefully. It was a relief. Perhaps they were over the illness already. Instead of waking them, she changed into a fresh gown, then settled down into a seat.

A little while later, Sybil stirred and rose.

"How were they through the night?" Jennet whispered.

"Your brother is somewhat better, but Ada was fretful most of the night."

"Well, I will keep watch now. Why don't you clean up and go to break your fast?"

Her friend must be exhausted after her vigil.

"Aye, I think that I do need some fresh air." Sybil dressed and fastened her chatelaine around her waist. Jennet didn't own one of the chain-link belts necessary to carry around trinkets because she rarely left home, and she didn't sew. For her, they seemed pointless. She'd rather have her bow, but it was like Sybil to be prepared for any emergency.

"I made a broth for her. It will help her if you can get her to drink it. I think your brother is well enough he doesn't need any. You should offer him the ale that's on the table."

"If she wakes I'll see to it that she drinks some."

Sybil nodded, and her gaze slid past Jennet to stare at the bed. She appeared haggard and worn down.

"Perhaps if you need some rest, Lord Roger will let you nap in his chamber."

"I think that's a good idea. I'll see if I can find him in the great hall," Sybil said as she brushed past Jennet and left the chamber.

She was afraid to ask but wanted to know. "Has Lord Roger's temper cooled?"

"Aye. He was more reasonable when he returned, but you should be glad you weren't here. He did ask after you."

"Thank you," she said.

Sybil nodded.

"Now, get some food and rest."

Her friend pivoted and retreated down the hall.

After she left, Jennet locked the door and moved onto the bed that her friend had vacated. The skies were dark and dreary as thunderstorms fell over the area, shrouding them in a cool, damp day. She fell asleep, but when she woke, Eddie and Ada were both stirring.

She rushed around seeing to her patients, ordering food and wiping their foreheads with wet rags to keep fever at bay. She was thankful that they weren't out in the worst of the weather. They both improved throughout the day as she told them stories and mended some stockings. She didn't push the drink on Ada because it smelled like bitter fruit. Perhaps the batch had steeped too long, so she sent for some fresh mead.

Sybil returned late in the afternoon.

"I brought some broth and drink," her friend said as she balanced a tray in her hands and bumped the door closed with her hip. It clicked in place.

"They're both sleeping again, but much improved."

"I will see to them for a while. Go down and eat. I'm sure you need to get out by now. I fell asleep in Roger's room and didn't intend to be away so long."

"Aye, I believe I will. And you do look better rested."

She hurried down the steps and took up a seat at the first available spot she saw in the great hall. From her vantage point, she could see her knight laughing and conversing with the guest of honor, Lord Marcus Debar, and their host. She looked forward to having him to herself tonight and hearing that deep amusement she knew was in his voice wash over her. She ate quickly, then ran back up to check on Eddie and Ada before heading to the bench in the garden.

When she arrived back in the room, Eddie was leaning over Ada, and Sybil was pacing.

"What's happened?"

"She's become delusional again. She's calling out to people who aren't here." Her brother was frantic with worry. He looked as if he'd aged by years in the last few days.

"I'll see to her," Jennet promised. "Why don't you go down to the village and see if you can find a healer before they close the gates for tonight? We still have a little bit of time before the bells ring for curfew."

He hesitated.

"You need some fresh air, and there is a break in the weather. I can see to her."

He rose and nodded. "I think we do need the healer."

When he was gone, Sybil came up beside her.

"Can you go tell Giric I won't be able to meet him tonight?" Jennet asked. "He's at the table by Lord Yves."

"Are you certain? I can watch her a while longer." The worry seemed to have drained Sybil's color. Her pallor looked almost as bad as Ada's, and she feared her other friend would fall ill soon.

"No. I'll stay until the healer comes."

Sybil nodded and turned toward the door. "I'll be back shortly," she called over her shoulder.

A few moments later, Ada still mumbled, but she had settled into a more peaceful slumber. In between the worry for her friend, Jennet's thoughts turned to Giric and how she would miss him this evening, but also that soon, they would have Eddie's acknowledgment, and they would be wed.

∾

The next morning, Giric woke alone in his bed, remembering the way he'd roused the day before. His cock hardened instantly. Although he'd quite liked waking with Jennet by his side and missed it this morning, he'd rushed from the bed yesterday to prevent himself from getting lost in her. It would have been so easy to kiss her, and he knew, in his aroused state, he'd have wanted to take things further.

He'd been disappointed when Sybil appeared by his side last night to inform him Jennet wouldn't be meeting him, but it had afforded him the opportunity to get to know his host a little better. He'd even been invited to an early morning tour of Lord Yves's land with a group of English nobles.

As they rode out, he took special notice of the landscape and the area where the melee would occur. Knowing the terrain would be useful when he made his move against Edward Linton. He'd not seen the man about yesterday. That was slightly concerning. What if Baron Bruton had seriously injured the man, and he didn't plan to participate in the last event of the tournament? Giric would have to find the man that morning and challenge him if he was standing out of the final competition. His plan wouldn't work if he couldn't capture the man.

Giric turned his attention to the man seated on a horse just ahead of him, the host of this extravagant gathering. Since Lord Yves lived so close to the Scottish border, King William wanted to know what kind of man the baron was. Giric had made some headway the day before in his assessment of his character.

The dark-haired English lord had a hard, chiseled visage and stood a good half-head taller than him. He reminded Giric of the tales he'd heard of Roman generals. In his research, he'd discovered that the baron was an experienced warrior, and although he was only in his early forties, he was widowed.

Lord Yves kept steely-eyed armed guards near his side at all times. He could be charming and was a gracious host, but his eyes were cold. Giric could see he held his secrets close and kept his enemies guessing.

Lord Yves was powerful and rich. Everyone present knew that by the pageantry of this tournament, but King William had wanted to know the man's heart. Giric had always been a good judge of character—that was why the king assigned him this mission. What lay beneath this man's aloof behavior, and was the granite layer behind his façade set in stone?

Knowing this was to be a short outing because Lord Yves had to get back early for the day's events, Giric trotted up next to him. "Ye have lovely land for it being in England. Must be because yer so close to yer Scottish neighbors," he jested.

"I prefer the air up here in the north. Perhaps your king would come to visit sometime or invite me to his court." The man smiled, calculated and reserved.

"I'm sure he'd be pleased to host ye."

"I haven't seen you in the jousts." His words were casual, but it was a question regardless of the feigned indifference. Giric knew the man was enquiring about his purpose here.

"Hand-to-hand combat is more to my liking. I'll be participating in the melee."

A large blond man with a crooked nose inched up beside them. Lord Yves nodded an acknowledgment to the newcomer then turned his attention back to their conversation.

"Ah, I like a man who knows his strengths and sticks with them. The king must be proud of his nephew."

Ah, so Lord Yves had researched him as well.

"Aye, I agree. What are yer strengths?"

"Taking care of my home and my people. It's important to

have your priorities in order when you live in a hostile environment."

He thought he understood what the man was saying. The lord was like a clan chief, and Giric knew this mentality. God, clan, country was a rule he lived by and, he respected anyone else who did the same. With just these few words, he was confident that he could tell King William that even if Lord Yves were planning a rebellion with King Richard's brother, in the end, he would side with whoever ensured his people and lands were well cared for.

Giric asked no more questions, and since Lord Yves apparently had meetings he needed to attend, their host left shortly after with his guards to return to the castle. Giric continued on with the others for a little while longer as they explored the rest of Lord Yves's land.

It was still early morning when he returned. After stabling his horse, Giric rounded a corner of the castle to see Edward Linton having a heated argument with the Earl of Bruton, the man who had unseated him in the joust.

How fortuitous to come across them and learn that Edward was healthy and whole after his defeat. Some pressure eased from his chest. He would be able to find his revenge, but he needed to know why these men were still arguing. Had they not left their differences on the jousting field? He moved closer but turned his back to them as he pretended to inspect the architecture of the castle.

"Have you told her yet?" the man asked Edward.

"No, I haven't had the opportunity. I cannot blurt out 'I'm going to force you to wed Roger.'"

"You have to tell her soon. I expect for us to wed here before we leave the tourney."

"Please, Roger. I have to approach this gently."

Giric peeked over his shoulder. Edward was drawn and pale. He held his hand to the stone wall to steady himself. Perhaps he had reinjured his leg when he'd lost the joust.

How was he to have a fair battle with the man if he were impaired? He squashed down the guilt he felt. He'd waited too long for this.

"I already told her we would wed." The earl stood rod straight, confident that he was in charge.

"And was she agreeable?" Edward shook his head as if he were confused.

"She said some nonsense about someone else courting her. Well, you have chosen, and the deal will be done." Lord Roger sounded cold as if he were selling cattle instead of choosing a wife. He'd be sorry for Edward's sister if she weren't his enemy's daughter.

"It's not that easy. You know our past." Edward's voice lowered, and he glanced around as if trying to keep a secret.

"Inside. Let's break our fast while we discuss the dowry." The earl ignored Edward's protest and marched off, fully expecting the baron's son to follow behind.

Roger Nash would be an awful husband to any lass unlucky enough to be tied to him…but that wasn't Giric's concern.

CHAPTER 11

*J*ennet was happy to see Ada had made some improvement during the morning. Enough so that Edward had finally left the room to get some air. Last night, the healer had wanted to blood-let her friend, but Jennet couldn't stand the sight and the coppery smell, so she had to tell the man no. Instead, he'd left herbs and instructed her to make a brew with it and hot water. She'd done so, but now that her brother's betrothed was able to sit up, Jennet wanted to get something else in her belly.

Even though little time had passed since they'd broken their fast, she sent Sybil down to procure some fresh mead, bread, and cheese. It was as much to get her fidgety friend out of the room as it was to help her sick one. Sybil had tossed and turned all night, keeping Jennet from sleeping, and she'd been pacing the morning hours away, twisting her hands around the links of her clanking chatelaine and causing Jennet's nerves to stand on end. When her friend did return, she'd probably send her away somewhere else, so she wouldn't be hovering like a stableman waiting for a mare to give birth.

As she waited for Sybil to return and watched the rising

sunlight, she wondered where Sir Giric was. She didn't want to lose another moment with him, but her friend came first. She was just contemplating sending him a message to come to her chamber when Sybil walked back into the room.

"How's she doing?"

"Much better," Ada answered, then winked at her.

Sybil froze at the sound of her voice. Her shoulders drooping, she trudged farther into the room. "Are you sure you should be up like this?"

"Aye. I'm feeling the worst has passed."

Sybil set the tray down on the table. "Well then, good. This should help." She picked up the glass nearest her, strolled over, and handed it to Ada.

Ada lifted it to her lips, and then her nose twitched, her cheeks pinching up as if it were sour. "It smells awful. Perhaps I was mistaken. I don't think my stomach is up for it yet."

"Let me see." Jennet reached for the cup and sniffed. "Argh. It smells like rotting plants. Is that what they gave you in the kitchens? I'll have to let the servant know the mead has gone bad." Rising, she walked over to the tray to set the cup down.

She picked up another cup and sniffed it. "This one smells sweet, normal." Grabbing the remaining one, she did the same. "This one is good as well."

Turning to Sybil, Jennet noticed she was fiddling with her belt again. "Will you stop that, please? The rattling is making my head ache."

Sybil froze and cupped her hands around her chatelaine as if she were hiding something.

Jennet's face paled. A memory flashed in her head. Ada drinking wine, then sharing it with Eddie, just before Sybil knocked the cup over. Trepidation flooded her like cold water was being dumped on her head. It slowly dripped to her toes as an awful suspension took root.

"What is that in your chatelaine?" Jennet asked.

Sybil stilled. Her eyes grew large, and she appeared to stop breathing as her gaze shifted from her to the floor then back again.

Jennet took a step closer and reached for Sybil's chatelaine. Her friend retreated. "Sybil. Why will you not show it to me?" She was confused, but the emotion quickly turned to mistrust. And she hated the feeling as it sludged through her veins.

"It's nothing." Sybil clipped the words and drew her shoulders back.

"Then let me see."

"It's just some drops for my eyes. The healer gave them to me before he left." She knew this was a lie. Sybil hadn't even been in the room when the man had come up from the village to see Ada last night.

"Belladonna?" She studied her friend's eyes. They bore no tell-tale sign of the drops used to entice men by making one's pupils appear enlarged. She had a vague understanding of what the nightshade plant could do to a person. They could make one's eyes look shiny and full.

Or they could be used as a poison.

She lunged and grabbed the vial on the belt. Sybil tried to swat her away, but Jennet was able to get her hand on it. Pulling it to her, a *snap* rent through the air when the small clasp holding it to the belt broke. Jennet opened the bottle and smelled.

"Did you put this in Ada's drink?" Anger and disbelief warred in her mind.

Shaking her head, Sybil backed to the door just as it swung open. Eddie and Lord Roger strode in. Her brother as solemn as when he'd heard the news of their oldest sibling's death and Lord Roger was wearing the closest thing to a smile she'd ever seen on the man. She focused her attention back on the woman in front of her, who had been her child-hood friend.

Sybil had tried to kill Ada.

Fury erupted from her throat as it vibrated and clawed through her. "Why?" she questioned, ignoring the men.

Chills spread down her back as her thoughts turned to the alley, a man coming at her and Ada with a knife. Glancing back and forth between them as if he weren't certain who to attack, then Sybil pulling her back and leaving Ada exposed.

Sybil shook her head. "No." The word was a squeak, barely audible.

"And in the village. You paid that man." She could hear the disbelief in her own voice, but the truth began to take shape in her mind.

Sybil hung her head, then turned as if she'd run from the room.

Eddie held his arm out, blocking her path. "What's going on here?" He shut the door and bolted it.

Jennet clenched her hand around the vial of poison. She'd never felt rage so raw. Pointing at Sybil, she let her gaze travel to the men. "She tried to kill Ada." A gasp escaped, and she pinned Sybil with the accusation. "Did you try to kill Eddie too?"

"No." Horror flashed on her face. "That was an accident. He took Ada's cup." Moisture pooled in Sybil's eyes, and she folded her arms around herself.

"Why?" This time the heated words came from her brother.

"Because you should have chosen me." Sybil tilted her chin up and drew her shoulders back.

"What?" He seemed genuinely perplexed. Sybil cringed and for a fraction of a moment, Jennet felt pity for her as tears welled and fell down her cheeks. Eddie had never noticed the way she worshiped him.

Sparing a glance over her shoulder, she saw Ada watching the affair, her own eyes wet with unshed tears, and her jaw slack in disbelief.

Sybil continued, "I'm an earl's daughter and a better match for you." Her face was fixed on Eddie's. She started toward him, and he held up a hand. Then her regard turned to Roger. "And I cannot live in his house another minute. I feel like a servant, and he plans—"

Lord Roger's voice was cold and clipped as he cut her off. "Well then, sister. I can remedy that. I will help the baron escort you to the village where we will meet with the magistrate. I am sure he has lodgings for you."

The earl's face was granite. It was as if he had no feelings for his sister at all, or perhaps she'd damaged his pride. Jennet couldn't imagine Eddie ever being so distant to her, but she'd never tried to murder someone.

"How could you? We were friends." Ada's voice trembled from behind her.

"I'm sorry, Ada. But I love him, and I'd be the better wife. I didn't want to hurt you."

"She must have paid the man in the village to attack me as well." Ada's gaze turned to Eddie. He nodded.

Sybil reached for Eddie again, but Roger clasped her arm and yanked her toward the door. "Let's take her to the village."

"Yes." Eddie's voice was frigid. "We should take her now." He hurried over to the bed and hugged Ada. Then he whispered something in her ear, and she nodded.

When he stood, Eddie glanced toward her. "Take care of her, Jennet."

"Aye, brother. I will."

She couldn't meet Sybil's eyes as the woman wailed, and Roger dragged her from the room.

When the door shut behind them, she turned to Ada to

see her face had gone pale. For a moment, Jennet was afraid she'd had more poison. "Are you feeling okay?"

"Aye, I'm just in disbelief. How could she have done such a thing? Sybil has always been so kind."

"I don't know. She's known for a long time that Eddie was enamored with you. I thought she was moving past her own infatuation. But something about her just seemed different and desperate this trip."

Ada threw back the covers and stood. "I'm feeling much better, but I think it will be good to get some fresh air and sun."

"Are you certain you have the strength?"

"If I'm confined to this room for any longer, I'll go mad. Especially if I think too hard about what Sybil has done."

"I agree then, but if you tire, we will return straightaway."

They made their way down to the fields and watched a couple rounds of jousting before heading back toward their chamber. Jennet had to admit that Ada's coloring did look better after the walk. Upon returning to the castle, they stopped to enjoy a small midday meal in the great hall. She was happy to see Ada's appetite had somewhat returned, and she was able to keep down some bread and sweet mead. Once they reached their chamber, they sat and talked while they worked on some mending and waited for the men to return.

But as they sewed, Jennet's mind couldn't stop processing the morning's events. Sybil's actions returned to the forefront of her mind. She felt as if she was missing something. Perhaps Eddie would have more details when he returned.

A little while later, her brother walked back in, thankfully without Lord Roger. His haggard appearance left no room for doubt that between dealing with Sybil and the lingering effects of the drug in his own body, he needed rest. She decided her questions could wait until he felt better, so she quickly excused herself and went hunting for her knight.

A fter thoroughly exploring the camp, Giric started back toward the fields to see if there was any sign of Edward Linton. He should have taken the opportunity to challenge him when he'd overheard the man with the earl, but the timing hadn't felt right. Tonight, Giric might have to visit Edward's room after the evening meal to issue the challenge. He worried that the man had been too injured by being unseated at the joust to participate in the melee.

Sun shone down on the jousting field, and the earth had dried from the rains of the previous day. He watched the tourney event with interest, studying the forms of all participating. Some performed well, but a few of the knights and noblemen appeared fatigued from participating for days on end. They were having a harder time hitting their marks today, but those that did were proving their skill to be superior.

By early afternoon, the sun blazed down with fiery intensity, and his patience was waning. Since there was still no sign of Edward Linton, he decided he could wait no longer. Giric couldn't risk that he would neglect the melee tomorrow. He was going to the man's room to find him now.

As he pivoted back toward the castle, his gaze caught on the lass who had headed his way. Jennet. She was breathtaking, smiling at the people she passed, offering greetings, but still moving straight toward the fields. She'd forgone a headpiece, and today her hair cascaded over her shoulders as a gentle breeze blew the silky strands and curved them into her body.

In a red gown, she lit the day with color that surely had everyone nearby watching her. When her gaze fell on him, she smiled—not just a slight grin that she'd given the guests as she passed, but one that brightened her eyes and filled her cheeks. It said to him that she'd missed him as he had her. Then she quickened her pace, and he knew that although he'd alluded to it with her before, he would not let the day pass without asking her to be his partner.

Striding toward her, he tamped the urge to pull her in his arms and swing her around. He would be able to do that soon enough. Perhaps they could wed tomorrow evening, after the fight. He would have his revenge, and then he would have the woman who had so quickly become everything he desired.

They came face-to-face, standing scant inches apart. Her cheeks were rosy, and her lips full, and his heartbeat accelerated with the thought of claiming her mouth again. He took her hand.

"I came as soon as I could. Have you missed me?" The amused teasing tone in her voice sounded like a chorus singing hymns in perfect tune.

"Aye, 'tis been too long since I've seen yer bonny face." And he was surprised to realize his words weren't a jest. Each moment without her had been filled with anticipation of when they would meet again.

"I have so much to tell you. Sybil has been taken to the local prison." She squeezed his hand as she shook her head.

"Nae. Why?"

"She tried to kill Ada," Jennet whispered, then shivered and glanced around to see if anyone heard her.

"Is she all right?" His insides tightened. Anger, concern, and disbelief warred in his head.

"Aye. She will be, but it's been a shock for us all."

"Why would she do such a thing?" He'd thought Sybil to be a kind person, but there were times she'd seemed abrupt and angry. Now he wanted even more to cocoon Jennet in his embrace, knowing she'd been so close to a viper. His grip tightened on her hand.

Her attention traveled around the crowds. "I don't want

to talk about it where others might hear. I'll tell you in private."

"Should we go to your chamber?" The thought of her in his reminded him of her in his tunic, her warm body beside his as she trailed her fingers across his chest.

"We can't go to my room. Although Ada is doing better, I fear she and Eddie may both be resting."

"We'll go to my chamber, then." And he would kiss her— he knew it—and his body tightened with the desire that surged through him stronger than the most potent Scottish spirits.

Once they breached the walls of the castle, he guided them through the great hall. "Have ye eaten?"

"Just a small meal with Ada a little while ago."

He stopped one of the baron's servers and requested that drink and refreshments be brought to his room. When they turned to go, she bumped into another server who carried a tray with a pitcher of ale on it. It splashed all over the front of her gown.

"I'm so sorry, my lady." The blushing young man's voice shook.

"No, it was my fault. It's nothing," she insisted.

When they reached his chamber, she walked right in, letting go of his hand and wrapping her arms around her chest. He turned and bolted the door.

"I'm glad I chose red today. Hopefully, this gown will not stain. It's more than I thought." She glanced down at the soaked fabric and shuddered.

"Would ye like a dry tunic to wear?" He hoped she did because he'd been sleeping with the one she'd worn. It smelled of her, exotic roses and sandalwood.

"Aye. Please. Perhaps this won't take too long to dry if I lay it out."

He reached into his trunk and took out the fresh garment. "Here. I'll turn while you change."

"Always gallant, Sir Giric." She grinned. It was a playful smile that tested the limits of his chivalry. His chest tightened with need at the direction his thoughts had taken him in.

"Aye, I will always see to yer wishes, Lady Jennet."

She blushed, and he swiveled to face the door before he was tempted to claim her lips. He'd not anticipated having her in his room again before they were wed, and now she'd be nearly naked. What had he been thinking?

His body ached with indecision and the hunger to claim her. Would that be moving too fast for her?

"I am done." Her throaty voice was like a soothing balm. If he weren't mistaken, he heard desire in its depths.

When he turned, his breathing stalled. This tunic fell just above her knees, leaving her calves, ankles, and feet exposed. He'd not had such a good view of her in the dark on the night she'd stayed in his bed. She'd removed her stockings, which he thought might not be necessary, but he was glad she'd chosen to do so. The sight of her bare skin had him wanting to rub his hands on the smooth flesh. Despite the shortness of the garment, it was too large and fell off one shoulder. He wanted to place kisses on that spot and work his way up to her mouth, draw her near, and feel her curves next to his body.

"Ye are going to undo me, lass."

She smiled, and he thought perhaps she was trying to seduce him. Her head tilted in an invitation, and she took a step forward.

A knock sounded at the door. He turned around and opened the portal to see the server from downstairs with a pitcher of mead, two glasses, and a tray of meats, cheese, and bread. Giric held his hand out for the offering without letting the man breach the frame. "I can take it. Thank ye."

The server handed it to him, pivoted, and was gone. Bolting the door, Giric turned and strode toward the table.

"Sit if ye wish." He motioned to a chair at the small table.

"I will, thank you."

He poured two glasses, then joined her. They ate as Jennet told him what had transpired with Sybil earlier in the day and how she'd also been responsible for the attack in the village.

"Will yer brother and friend have any lasting effects from the poison?"

"No. They are already much improved."

"I'm glad to hear it."

"This mead is delicious." She licked her lips, and he wanted to groan, but she wasn't even his yet.

He could wait no longer. Kneeling in front of her, he took her hand in his.

"I wanted to talk to yer brother first, but I haven't had my chance." He took in a deep breath as her gaze rested on him, eyes twinkling and bright.

"He will be well rested later, and I can take you to him."

"I wish for ye to be my wife." He held his breath, fear suddenly spiking in his chest. If she said no, he would survive, but he knew he'd be leaving a huge part of his heart in England when he returned home.

Her free hand stretched out and caressed his cheek. The gentle strokes sent waves of sensation spiraling down to his core. "I would like that." She nodded.

"Will yer brother approve? He has no' even met me yet."

"He will let me choose. Ada already spoke to him, and he said yes."

"Do ye choose me?"

"Aye, Giric. I choose you."

He couldn't contain the joy that burst from inside, and he was on his feet before he knew what he was doing. Wrapping Jennet in his arms, he drew her up and twirled her around, savoring the feel of her, her musky-sweet scent, and the way she giggled. Jennet held on as if she'd been waiting for him to ask her.

"I must meet yer brother because 'tis proper for me to secure his permission as well."

"He'll be pleased to meet you and know that I have chosen such an honorable knight."

He eased down onto the chair and pulled her into his lap. Her bonny brown eyes landed on him, and he couldn't help himself. "I'm going to kiss ye."

"Please." Her breathless reply wrapped around his chest and his pulse beat louder.

He took her mouth in his, and it was like no other kiss he'd had before. Jennet was going to be his wife. The raw sensation that gripped him had his groin tightening, begging the rest of his body to lay her out and claim her now. As her tongue swiped across his, he knew this was right, that they belonged together, and fate had found a way to see their paths had crossed. He forgot everything except this moment, the fulfillment and joy he felt holding her in his arms.

She drew back, her face inches from his. "Shall we marry tomorrow?"

"Aye. As soon as the melee is done."

"Oh, and you'll want to talk to my brother about my dowry first. When you meet him tonight, we can make the arrangements."

"Nae, I want ye. If ye have a dowry, it would be helpful for us and the clan, but 'tis no' necessary."

Strands of music drifted under the doorway and through the air. He didn't know where it came from, but it was just enough to lend an additional hint of magic to the moment.

"Dance with me." She jumped up and drew him to his feet.

"Aye."

And it was like that first night. They performed the same fluid movements, and when his hand met hers, the sizzle was still there, but this time magnified, as if they were the shore and the sea, neither able to exist without the other.

As they progressed through the steps, their bodies melded together, too close to be proper in public. This was the most intimate thing he'd ever done with a woman. It was as if their souls were connecting as their eyes remained locked, and heat built inside him.

When the strains of the music faded, she twined her fingers with his, and her dilated eyes studied him as she took in a deep breath. Her flushed cheeks turned pinker, her mouth fell open, and she inhaled before saying, "Make me your wife now."

His core tightened, every muscle in his body taut like the bow she wielded with precision. In such a short time, she'd mastered him as well. Emotions flooded him: desire, ecstasy, but most of all, love. This was what her parents had possessed, and now he knew why they'd risked everything to keep it. He couldn't imagine Jennet in another's arms.

She was his, and he belonged to no other.

He nodded, not having the words to express the sensations swamping his senses. Instead, he scooped her into his embrace and held her there, cherished her, before covering her mouth with his.

CHAPTER 12

*W*hen the music started, Jennet had known this was the right time for them to make a commitment to each other. The need she felt was so thick and heavy that she was drowning in it, and only clinging to him would save her. Even before she'd gotten to know him, there was something familiar, like fate was bringing them together to complete the other.

Giric was everything she'd ever wanted in a husband. His honor was unshakable and real, he put family above all else, and he made her laugh. Not only that, he valued her opinions and wasn't afraid to let her make choices. The freedom and bliss she felt in his arms were what she'd searched for since losing her independence all those years ago.

Her Scottish knight was her liberator, and now he would be her husband. She wanted this bond with him, wanted it so deeply that the emotions reached into her chest, and it threatened to bust.

His lips closed on hers, honey and mead filling her senses. She was lost in this moment, this man, and what her world was going to be. She'd be going to Scotland to live with Giric, and that didn't terrify her as it would have only last week. It liberated her, knowing that she would be there with a man she could trust. They would make new memories and have their own family.

As she lay cradled in his arms, his tongue tangled with hers, she was vaguely aware of Giric moving. Anticipation surged as she held on to him. He lowered her to the bed, gently peeled his arms from her, and stood.

"Are ye sure ye are ready?" His husky Highland burr washed over her, and gooseflesh rose on her arms.

"Aye. I've never wanted anything more. I want this. I want us."

She thought a rumble might have come from his throat, but her heart was beating so loudly she wasn't certain. All she knew was that Giric was the man she'd been praying for her whole life, even before she'd known his face or his smooth voice. Her body had known as soon as they'd touched on that first night.

He licked his lips and watched her a moment. Seeming to weigh the consequences of what they were about to do. He reached for the bottom of his tunic and pulled it over his head. His bare chest boasted muscles that rippled with each movement. It was why she'd felt so secure in his arms.

As he tugged at his breeches, she shimmied the tunic she wore up around her hips, then sat up and drew it off. She experienced a shock of fear, thinking she might not be all he wanted, but one glance at his reaction told her she was wrong. She eased onto her back as his gaze fixed on her as if she were a glass of wine after going days without a drink.

He climbed onto the bed next to her, and his weight had her body shifting into his. The awareness of his flesh next to hers heated her as new sensations flooded her senses. She breathed him in. Need enveloped her.

His fingers caressed her cheek, and he spoke. "I promise to put you above all else. You will be my family now, and I will care for you with everything I have in me."

"And I will do the same."

His hand trailed to her neck as his mouth once again melded with hers. His fingers traveled farther down and gently took hold of her breast. Need exploded in her, and she arched into his touch. This seemed to spur him on because his kiss became more fevered, and he caressed her flesh again before moving to her belly, where he traced circles on the flat surface.

She giggled into his mouth, and then his hand dipped again. His fingers reached the spot between her legs, and her laughter turned into a gasp, as they moved up and down in the slickness that had pooled there. A moan escaped as pleasure engulfed her. He continued the sweet torture until she was almost panting with something she couldn't name, a precipice she'd never experienced, and she shifted her hips into his palm to increase the pressure.

Giric withdrew then, and she thought to protest, but he moved too swiftly. Drawing her legs apart, he rose up, then settled between them. When the warm, smooth tip of his manhood touched her core, she moaned at the sensation. He slid the length up and down her passage before stopping and looking directly into her eyes, her soul, her whole being.

Then he breached the opening and seated himself deep within her core. There was a brief moment of pain, but she didn't care because everything else about it felt so right. He stilled and dipped so that his lips were on hers, and she kissed him with everything she had in her. Her heart was nearly bursting with love for this man.

As they kissed, his hips started to rotate slowly. He didn't pull out as much as he rubbed back and forth, reaching the deepest part of her as his pelvis rocked back and forth on the nub at her center. Heat and desire surged in waves as she fought to catch her breath, but at the same time, she sensed her body tilting farther up toward his, asking for more.

Pulses of pleasure burst in her core, and everything else

disappeared as the swells of sensation hit her again, and then again, and then she gave into them as they came faster, harder, and stronger. She was vaguely aware that mewling sounds might be escaping her throat.

As the last of the pulses hit her, Giric leaned up on his arms and gazed down at her. He pulled out, then thrust forward. He repeated the process, once, twice, three times, then he seemed to be falling into that same place where she'd just been. Out of reality, out of time, and in that space that belonged to only them.

Moments later, he shifted to the side and pulled her into the crook between his arm and shoulder. As she lay nestled there, enjoying the peace and security, she said, "I'd like to do that again soon."

He placed a gentle kiss on her forehead, then whispered, "My lovely Jennet, ye have made me the happiest man in all of the word. And once we are wed, nothing is stopping us from doing it every day, or three times a day." He laughed.

"Will we go to Scotland straight away, or will we be able to retrieve my belongings? Oh, I need to say goodbye to my father, and I'd like for you to meet him."

"If that is what ye wish, we will visit yer family before I take ye to yer new home."

"Yes. It is."

Her thoughts turned to how pleased her father would have been about this match if he'd retained his senses, but she still had to let him know that she'd found a man who put her above all else. Perhaps that would give him some solace before he left this world. Peace claimed her as she lay in Giric's arms.

~

J ennet snuggled into him, and her soft weight went slack. It was a first for him, to let a woman fall asleep in his arms, and he had a feeling he'd never get enough of having her by his side.

Tilting his head toward her, he inhaled her rose and sandalwood scent. It was heady, and he reveled in the realization that she was now totally and completely his. In her arms, he felt as if he had everything that he'd been missing all these years. He relaxed, visions of their life together playing in his head as a sweet slumber fell over him.

He dreamed of the day his father died, the girl with the bow, the smoldering pile of the inn when his cousins had finally taken him in search of his father. Then the worst of the images assailed him, pulling the charred remains of two adults and a child from the destroyed building.

He woke in a sweat, his lungs burning from the memory of inhaling the noxious fumes. Jennet was still nestled next to him, and he drew her near, welcoming the comfort of her presence.

The sunlight had begun to fade. He'd forgotten his mission and spent the afternoon lost in her. Och, hell, how was he to take care of her when he couldn't even fulfill the mission to avenge his father's death? He had to find Edward Linton and make certain the man would be in the melee tomorrow. It was the only fair way to seek his retribution.

Reluctantly, he pulled free of his woman, the lady that would be his wife. His chest soared at the thought. Once this business was over tomorrow, they could start their life together.

But first, he had to bury the past and move on.

He dressed, then leaned over the bed to wake her with a long sweet kiss. "Jennet, I have to see ye to yer room."

She blinked, then sat up with the covers pulled to her

chest. "Are you so eager to meet my brother you must wake me?" She grinned, and it was a beautiful sight.

As she rose to dress, he couldn't help but gaze upon her lovely form. He wished he could change his mind and ask her to lay back down and never leave his room. And tomorrow night he could, but now he had to finish his quest.

"I want to meet with him, but 'twill have to wait until after the melee. It's late now, and I need to seek out the man who I'll be challenging tomorrow."

She frowned. "Are you sure this is what your father would want? Perhaps he would wish for you to look to the future."

"I'm taking care of both at the same time. I'll meet you in the great hall as soon as I have won tomorrow, and my demands have been agreed to. Then we can have yer brother escort us to the chapel."

"I will let you, but only because I need to check on Ada. You have to make me two promises." She wrapped her arms around him.

"And what are those, fair lady?"

She drew back and held up a finger. "Number one. You will return to me uninjured."

"Aye. I'm good with a sword and think I can manage that one. What's the other?"

She reached into a hidden pocket on her gown and pulled out a small square of cloth. "You must take this with you."

It was a kerchief with gold and blue flowers and leaves embroidered around the edges. "Wear it boldly because 'tis the only public favor I have ever offered a knight."

He placed his palm on his chest. "I will wear it here, next to my heart."

"All right then, husband-to-be, you may escort me to my room, and I will find you on our bench when the melee is done."

He left her in the hall just outside her door with a kiss. He wanted to meet her brother but couldn't spare the time. He had to find his enemy's son.

As he turned to go, excitement consumed him. Tomorrow, he would have the revenge he'd always wanted, and a wonderful lady for a wife. Fate had finally dealt him a winning hand.

CHAPTER 13

*J*ennet woke to a soft glow indicating that the sun was about to make its climb in the sky. Ada was already dressed and sitting up in a chair by the table, putting needle to a kerchief she was embroidering. The blue and gold thread she used matched the one Jennet had given to her knight. Ada had insisted she must make one with their house colors since she would soon be part of the family.

A smile broke across Jennet's face as she realized she'd be making one with Giric's clan's colors soon or perhaps even one with a lion for the king he served. The thought of going to Scotland should have been scary, but she found herself excited by the prospect.

"You are up early."

"Aye. Edward and I have done nothing but rest for the past couple of days. I needed to move about."

"You look so much better today. How are you feeling?"

"Almost normal." Her friend smiled.

Jennet stretched, climbed from beneath the covers, and began to dress. "Good. You and Eddie were sleeping when I came in last night. Where is he?"

Ada's improved health meant she could be left unobserved for a few moments, but Eddie had been reluctant to leave her side. He'd decided to stay in their room last eve, possibly so he could keep his guard up around his soon-to-be wife. Jennet also surmised he didn't want Ada in here alone after all the excitement.

"He went to get some food to break our fast."

"Sir Giric and I want to wed today. I need to talk to him so that I can introduce them. It's taken too long for them to meet."

"When I asked the other day, Edward was eager to meet the man who'd captured his sister's heart."

She blushed. "Has it been that obvious?"

"Aye. It has." Ada laughed.

"I wonder what's keeping Eddie." She fidgeted. Her nerves were on end. Worry over what was going on with Giric plagued her. "What time does the melee start?"

"Soon, I believe."

Something else had been bothering her. She needed to understand Sybil's motivations. It was so unlike her. She still felt as if there was something to Sybil's actions that she was missing.

"Och, talking to him will have to wait until after then. Tell him I must see him and not to leave the room until I get back."

"Where are you going?"

"To the village. I won't be long, but something is bothering me. I'll tell you when I get back." She opened the door and ran out before Ada could protest.

Shortly into her talk with Sybil, she heard the trumpets sound, indicating the melee had started. She breathed in deeply and said a quick prayer for Giric's safety.

~

After escorting Jennet to her room, Giric had gone to bang on Edward Linton's door. The man didn't answer. He repeated the process several times during the night, at one point picking the lock to see if the man's belongings were still in the chamber. He tried again in the morning after a fitful sleep. Frustrated, Giric had made his way to the great hall to wait for dawn, hoping the man would make an appearance before the melee could begin.

Luck was with him.

A little while later, Edward strolled into the hall, looking better than he had the day before. Color had returned to his cheeks, and his limp appeared to have the same quality as it had when Giric had seen the man upon his arrival. Good. He would have felt a twinge of guilt at challenging a man who was injured.

The hall was crowded with knights and nobles seeking to break their fast before the fighting began. The audience was perfect for his purpose. Edward wouldn't be able to refuse the challenge in front of so many.

He marched toward his enemy's son as the man talked to a servant. He appeared to be ordering food to be delivered somewhere. When the man turned to leave, Giric blocked his way.

"Pardon me," Edward said as he attempted to sidestep him.

"Nae." Giric cut off his path.

Raising his voice so that anyone nearby could hear, he called, "Edward Linton, son of the Baron of Gillingham. I challenge you to hand-to-hand combat in the melee."

The hall hushed, and although he kept his stare rooted on Edward's shocked brown eyes, he could sense almost every person in the room had stilled and waited for the reply.

Edward blinked, then squinted at him as he tried to understand what Giric was saying. "Who are you?"

"I am Giric de Beaumont MacDonald. And yer father killed mine. I demand that ye meet me on the field to answer for his crimes."

"My father has never slain anyone. You are mistaken." Edward's face shaded a vivid red.

"Eleven years ago, was yer father no' in Scotland? Did he cause a fire at a home of an innkeeper and his daughter?"

Edward turned the color of paste. Then he leaned in and whispered, "Ye are mistaken. He was there, but that is not what happened."

Giric didn't want to hear excuses. He wanted justice. He pulled the glove from his hand and threw it at Edward's feet. Either the Englishman would be proved a coward, or Giric would have his vengeance before the sun set.

"I expect to see ye on the field so that you may answer for yer father's crimes."

The man's gaze traveled the length of the room, skimming the myriad of faces as all of them watched Giric's challenge unfold. Edward swallowed.

His enemy's son pulled his shoulders back and met Giric's gaze straight on. Their eyes locked as Edward's strong will clashed with his own. Edward would be a formidable opponent.

Reaching down, Edward picked up the gauntlet, tacitly accepting the challenge.

"I will wait for ye on the east end of the field. There we will meet and settle this score."

"I will line up with the *tenans* since you are Scottish." Edward stood tall as he tossed the glove back to Giric and indicated that he would take the field on the side of the locals who held the land.

Giric caught his gauntlet. "Aye. I'll be with the *venans*." It was the first time he'd used the French word for those who come from afar to challenge.

Satisfied, Giric turned and strode from the room to fetch

his squire and prepare, leaving the baron's son to make his arrangements.

CHAPTER 14

*A*n hour and a half after walking in to see Sybil, Jennet walked out with the answers she'd been after, and while she'd never be able to forgive Sybil, she was glad she'd made the journey to talk to her old friend.

She paused in the great hall to break her fast because she'd missed the morning meal and her stomach was rumbling. When she finally strode back into the room, it was to find Ada's face red from crying, an uneaten meal laying cold on the table, and Eddie nowhere to be seen.

"What's wrong?" she asked as fear snaked its way into her breast.

"Edward is fighting in the melee."

She froze. Chills spread over her, and her hands began to tremble.

"Nae. Why would he do such a thing?"

"I don't know."

"They don't use blunted weapons in the melee." Her voice shook, and even as she made the statement, she realized Ada was probably already aware of that fact.

Dread pierced her heart as she thought about her brother

putting himself in such danger. He was good with a sword. She didn't doubt his skill, but he'd been sick for nearly two days and although he'd done a good job at hiding it, he had been injured the day before that.

"What did he say?"

"He only sent word that we shouldn't leave the room and that he'd be back when the battle was done."

Now Jennet wished she'd skipped the food below. Her gut twisted.

"I have to get down there. Perhaps there is a way to stop it." She closed her eyes and took a deep breath to build her courage.

But she knew the battle had started long ago. On her return from the village, she'd heard the clangs of swords, the screams of men, and the shouts of both victory and defeat. There would be nothing she could do, short of running onto the field to save her brother, and he'd never forgive her if she caused such a scene. She wouldn't storm the melee, but she had to go see if he was safe.

She bolted from the room before Ada could object.

Minutes later, she entered the area roped off from the rest of the field where family and friends could wait for news of their loved ones. The space was called the refuge, but to her, it was hell. Lord Yves's men had forced her in this direction, saying ladies weren't allowed on the field. Her heart beat so fast she could feel it, and her nerves were shattered.

Wounded men lay everywhere with others standing triumphantly over them and waiting for some price to be paid for their victory. Her belly roiled at the coppery smell that wafted through the air. She had to look but averted her gaze from each injured man as soon as she'd confirmed they weren't her brother.

The blood brought back terrifying images from the past, and her whole body began to tremble. She'd been there when her mother had died from a difficult childbirth. She'd been present when her older brother had lost his life at the hands of her uncle. She'd been helpless both times, and now that same despair was closing in around her.

And just like before, there was nothing she could do but watch as the people she loved most died in front of her.

～

Giric galloped across the field, the blare of the trumpet still resonating in his ears as he fixed his focus on the man charging from the other direction on his own steed. Edward Linton's horse had the colors of his house, blue and gold, draped across its back. Giric had sent his squire as a scout earlier to make sure he knew what to look for and could make haste toward the correct man. He didn't want to have to bother with the rest of the participants in the battle.

He respected Edward. The man hadn't flinched and had met Giric's challenge with the honor of a true knight despite his position as a baron's son.

He was mere yards from his target when another man from the *tenans* riding a destrier changed direction and shot toward him. He recognized the attacker. He was the blond with the crooked nose who had listened to his conversation with Lord Yves. He wore red and black and as he rode near, he aimed a spear at Giric's mount. Giric veered off course to protect his warhorse, but the sharp turn threw him off balance. He was nearly unseated from the unexpected attack.

The attacker circled about and charged again. This time, his blow connected with Giric's shield, the force so strong he was knocked sideways. The red and black knight was thrown from his horse at the impact. He rolled when he fell and stood almost immediately. The man drew his sword and started on foot toward Giric.

Giric jumped from his warhorse to meet the brute head-on. He couldn't focus on Edward until this threat was gone. The man hurtled at him with sword drawn.

"I dinnae wish to fight ye. I am here to battle another." Giric blocked the blow as the familiar-looking man struck.

"Aye, you may not wish to, but I think I could win a hefty purse for returning the queen consort's nephew to the Scottish king."

He'd purposely been reserved this week and not participated in the jousts to avoid bringing notice upon himself. But now he recognized this man. He had ridden nearby as Giric and Lord Yves had talked on their short ride in the country. Giric hadn't counted on others knowing who he was, nor that they may be seeking to make a profit on his head. And the man was right. His aunt and the king—not to mention his brother, the Lord of the Isles—would pay a handsome reward for his safe return.

The knight swung again, aiming for Giric's arm, a place that would wound him but surely not cause death. Giric deflected the blow with his own sword, and a *clang* rent the air. As he lifted his weapon to come back to a defensive pose, he caught a glimpse of Edward on the ground, occupied in his own battle with a man nearly twice his girth.

"This is yer last chance to walk away. I dinnae wish to harm ye, and I have business to see to."

"Aye. It will be seeing to your wounds when I'm done with you." The red-and-black knight cackled.

"So be it." Giric knew he would not make it to his goal until this man had been dealt with.

He swung, and they were locked in battle, both alternating blows, then deflecting. He scored a solid hit to the man's arm, but the knight's chainmail prevented any damage except bruising.

They circled each other, and Giric caught a glimpse of his enemy's son. Edward stepped awkwardly, and his leg gave beneath him. He fell to the earth with a clang as his armor rattled at the impact.

Giric had no idea who the man above Edward was, but the green-and-white attacker struck at the downed Edward's face with his fist. Edward attempted to get to his feet.

The red-and-black knight attacking Giric lunged again, and this time hit his side. The impact brought him back to the immediate danger. Giric couldn't save his mission, or Edward, until he fought off the man determined to bring him down.

The red and black knight charged again, but this time, instead of deflecting the threat, Giric slid to the side. His opponent lost his balance and stumbled forward. Giric came down and sliced the blade of his sword across the back of the man's thigh, where his armor didn't protect the sensitive flesh. His opponent fell to the ground as blood streamed from the wound.

Giric watched for a moment to assess the damage. The knight writhed on the ground, holding onto his injury. It was a deep cut, but the knight quite likely would live, though he'd never be the same.

Turning back to his original target, Giric spotted the other knight pulling the helmet from Edward's head. As it slid off, Giric saw that Edward was dazed and couldn't focus on his opponent. Blood dripped from his mouth. The attacker's helm allowed a good view of the man's twisted grin. He said something to Edward, but from his position, the words were inaudible to Giric. Then the other knight drew back with the axe.

The arse was going to kill him.

"Nae," Giric yelled.

Edward's attacker turned his attention toward Giric for a brief moment, then shook his head and continued to raise the weapon.

Giric reacted on instinct, charging the man and knocking him off Edward. The ax flew through the air and landed a few feet away. They rolled, and the attacker managed to land on top. The crazed knight drew back with his arm and came down hard with a fisted gauntlet on Giric's helm. The punch slid off to the side, but the impact was brutal, and a buzz vibrated in his ears.

Giric blinked, then took a quick deep breath. Drawing on his reserves and his training, he focused on getting the larger man off of him. Giric lifted his leg, swung it to the side, then planted his foot behind the attacker's ankle, pinning it in place. Then he pushed up with his other leg as he rose with his hip and flipped the man onto his back.

The man in green and white threw his arms in the air to knock Giric off, but Giric remained seated on the man's chest, keeping him pinned to the ground. As he blocked punches, Giric was able to reach behind his thigh and pull free the dirk he kept strapped to the back of his leg. His gloved hand almost dropped it when the man landed a jab to Giric's face.

He secured his grip, then leaned down and plunged the knife into the man's thigh where his chainmail didn't protect him. A furious roar came from the injured man's chest. Giric withdrew the blade.

The green-and-white knight bucked and swung again, throwing his pelvis into Giric and almost knocking him off. As he continued to struggle, Giric managed to grasp the edge of the gorget on the man's helm, pull it up, and plunge the knife between his breastplate and helm. The man stopped fighting and reached for his neck, writhing in pain.

Climbing off the man, who Giric guessed would no longer be a threat, he turned his attention to Edward. The baron's son remained prone and dazed on the ground. Giric had only just been in time to save his life.

Lifting the injured Englishman, he lay Edward across his

horse, then gathered his own warhorse. Giric made his way toward the refuge to see who would be there to bargain with. He was prepared to hand Edward over in exchange for the baron.

Victory was at hand.

CHAPTER 15

*J*ennet rushed through the refuge, looking for any sign of her brother or her Scottish knight. Her pulse pounded, and every part of her ached by the time Lord Roger stepped out in front of her. She didn't want to see him right now, but he might be her best hope of finding Eddie.

"Lord Roger." She curtsied, and he took her trembling hand.

"Ah, Lady Jennet. It is good to see you today." Plastered on his face was a smug smile that she could only describe as victorious.

She shivered and tried to pull away, but he held tight. "I must find my brother. Have you seen him?"

"I'm afraid it's not good news." Roger shook his head.

Her heart fell into her belly, and her breath stilled.

She shook her head, and her eyes began to sting, but before she could ask, he continued, "He has been captured."

She inhaled. He was alive.

"But there is no need for you to worry. I am taking care of everything. I have arranged the trade."

"What trade?" She drew her shoulders back and yanked her fingers free.

"I will give the barbarian yer ailing father in exchange for Edward. I doubt the brute knows your sire is on death's door anyway."

She gasped.

"No. You can't make that decision." Her worry transformed into fury, and her hands fisted. He had no right to bargain away her father.

"Has Edward not told you?"

She shook her head, afraid to hear what was about to spill from Lord Roger's overbearing lips.

"Ah, he has been quite busy." Roger picked at his nails, then put his hands by his sides before meeting her gaze. "He and I made an arrangement. You are to become my wife tonight, so I am the only one here who can bargain for his safe return."

"What?" Her stomach twisted, and her fingers shook with a combination of dread and anger.

"You are *not* my betrothed." She could feel the heat rising in her chest. "Eddie wouldn't do that to me."

"Aye, he would. We jousted over it, and I won. He had no choice but to relent. Besides, you and I will suit well." Was that why Eddie had been foolish enough to take on Lord Roger?

Would her brother do such a thing? There had been something he'd wanted to tell her before he and Ada fell ill, something he'd known she wouldn't be pleased with. How had he done this? She was supposed to be free to make her own choice.

This was all wrong, and she had to find Eddie and tell him this match was impossible. She had her heart set on Giric.

"I cannot marry you. I love another."

Roger's face hardened. "That doesn't matter. You will be my obedient wife. The bargain was struck."

"No. Where is Eddie? He can set this right. I will not marry you."

"You will, and if you expect me to free him from the Scottish knight, you will stop arguing now. We shall go back to the castle, draw up the paperwork, and send for your father straightaway." His hand clasped her arm, digging in and pulling her toward the castle.

She didn't fight as Lord Roger's words clawed at her, as the weight of them settled on her chest. Her breath stilled, and her body went numb. She felt ill.

"Scottish knight?" she asked as her whole being began to tremble.

"Aye. The man who captured Edward. His name is Giric de Beaumont MacDonald. He has ties to the Scottish throne."

No. She couldn't believe it. The world tilted, and she thought for a moment, she might fall to the ground. Lord Roger had to be mistaken, but pieces of their conversations started to fall into place.

She had to find Giric. This couldn't be true. Her honorable knight wouldn't do this to her.

Taking a deep breath, she asked, "Where are they?"

"At the west end of the refuge, but you don't need to see that right now. The sight is not fit for a gentle lady. I will escort you back, and we'll take care of everything."

"No." She pulled her arm free and ran for her brother and her knight.

~

The sun was now high in the sky, and the heat bit into Giric as he waited for word that the Earl of Bruton had sent for Edward Linton's father. Lord Roger Nash claimed he could speak on the family's behalf by virtue of being betrothed to Edward's sister. Although still dazed, Edward didn't protest the claim.

A small bit of doubt crept in at not dealing directly with the Linton family, but Giric had heard the conversations where an arrangement had been made. He knew the tale to be true.

"I had some ale brought. Drink this." Giric handed the glass to Edward, who was just starting to seem lucid again. Blood had seeped from the man's split lip to his blue-and-gold surcoat. Although he was only mildly injured, the blood loss made him appear as if he could be on death's doorstep.

"Why did you challenge me?" Edward's words were slightly slurred.

"I told ye. My father was killed by yer sire."

"No. That couldn't be true. He hates violence." Edward shook his head in a truly impressive display of disbelief.

"It is."

As time ticked by, he wondered if he'd have assurances in writing by the evening so that he could find Jennet. He longed to hold her in his arms. Reaching beneath his armor, he drew out the kerchief she'd given him. He held it to his nose and inhaled. Although his sweat now tainted it, the rose and sandalwood scent still lingered.

Edward's eyes sharpened and focused in on the cloth. "Where'd you get that?"

He smiled and held it over his heart. "From the lady that I intend to marry."

Edward's head tilted, and he appeared confused again. "And what is this lady's name?"

He almost didn't say, but he felt a respect for this man, who had been brave enough to meet him on the field and attempt to set matters right.

"Jennet." Just saying her name felt like repeating a sacred oath that made his insides quaver with anticipation.

The color in Edward's cheeks drained, and his jaw fell open.

"You are the Scottish knight." The words left Edward's lips, but they were almost a whisper, and if they hadn't been close, Giric wouldn't have heard.

"Aye. I'm Scottish."

"And you wish to marry the lass that belongs to." Edward nodded at the material.

"Aye. She has agreed."

"After today, she will change her mind." There was steel in the man's voice now, a certainty that hadn't been there before.

Giric blinked as dread forked through him. How would this man know such a thing? Something cold took root in his chest.

"Nae. We have already agreed." He traced the gold and blue flowers she'd sewn with her dainty hands. His eyes caught on the initials she'd stitched in the corner, "JL."

"But that was before you challenged her brother and held him ransom for her father's life."

Giric's throat closed, and his eyes blurred as he again took note of the colors on Edward's tunic. They were the same as the cloth in his hand, except they were now stained with blood.

This was Eddie.

His victory turned bitter and hollow.

CHAPTER 16

*J*ennet broke free from Roger and ran for her brother. The earl was wrong or playing some jest on her. He was angry at her for her refusal of his offer.

But when she reached the edge of the refuge, she saw Giric sitting on the ground. She almost smiled until she noticed he was holding her kerchief. He shook his head, and she followed his intent eyes as they landed on her brother.

Edward's surcoat was covered in blood. The contents of her stomach threatened to spill. Her feet carried her forward, but something in her screamed for her to stop and turn around. A voice inside pleaded with her to sprint back to the castle and forget what she'd seen and heard.

Giric glanced up and saw her. He covered his face, then ran his hands through his hair as if he were trying to deny what was plain before her.

He stood and reached out to her. She backed as tears streamed down her cheeks. She thought to wipe them away, but what good would it do? She knew they wouldn't cease. His gaze traveled between her and Eddie.

Her eyes rested on Giric and stayed as her heart jumped

to the next conclusion. She'd been part of his plan. Her heart split in two at that moment. The faith she'd placed in this man shattered like pottery. She'd trusted her freedom to him. She'd given him her heart.

She opened her mouth to speak, but the words refused to dislodge from her tongue. Then talons were again gripping her arm, and she found Lord Roger at her side. She turned to him and attempted to pull free, but his grip was firm.

"Unhand her." The snarl came from Giric.

Grounded and filled with anger at Lord Roger, she was able to turn back to her knight, who now had his fingers curled around the hilt of his sword like he was ready to unsheathe it and attack at any moment. She felt helpless; all her independence gone in one moment.

She would have to marry Lord Roger, and Giric was going to take his revenge on her family.

What had he said that night in his bed?

"I want the baron's family to suffer as mine has."

She uttered the awful conclusion. "I was part of your plan." Her voice shook, and her throat closed as a sob escaped. When her knees wobbled, she would have fallen had the earl not been holding her up.

He was her knight. He'd saved her and proven she could trust him. She'd freely given him everything—her favor, her faith, her body.

Had it been his plan to break her heart, or had he just intended to use her to get to Eddie and her father?

"Jennet." Giric inched forward again, his eyes confused. As if he'd not known who she was. Pretending to care…as if he'd not been trying to destroy her family all along. And the worst part of it was, she wanted him to wrap her in his arms and tell her it was all a mistake. She wanted to believe in the man who had harmed her brother and desired to see her father dead. What was wrong with her?

"No." She held up the palm that wasn't detained by Roger's grip.

"I didnae ken. I swear, I didnae." His voice sounded lost in the shouts that continued on around them.

She shook her head. He was lying. He had to be.

Lord Roger cut in. "Come, Jennet. I have already worked out the details."

"No. Let go of me. You have no say in this matter." She tried once more to pull free.

"Tell her, Edward. We are to be wed. We have a deal." His glare darted between Eddie and her.

She let her gaze travel to her brother, who couldn't meet her eyes. Bile rose in her chest. It was true. Eddie had taken away her choice, the one thing she'd always been assured was in her own hands. Not that it mattered now, anyway. She'd chosen poorly.

Giric was not the man she'd believed him to be.

Pulling back her shoulders, she tried to preserve some kind of dignity, but it was truly too late because she felt like a ship beaten by the waves and rocks of a treacherous shore. Now she floated about without sails, devoid of a purpose, lost. These three men had taken from her what had been promised.

Her gaze locked on Giric. "Was I part of your revenge? Did you take me to your bed to get back at my family?" She choked out the words.

Giric shook his head.

The grip on her arm tightened to a painful pinch, and she felt Roger stiffen.

Her chest burned as if a fire had been set within its walls. "You are just like my uncle. You have let revenge consume you and destroy everything."

Giric stepped forward and reached out with the hand that had held her so gently just the day before. "Jennet." Her name left his lips, and what stung the worst was that she still wanted to run to him.

He looked as if he wished to stroke her cheek and tell her that all would be well and that he would care for her. How had he become so good at lying? She gave him one last chance.

"Let Eddie go."

"Ye dinnae ken what ye ask." His eyes hardened.

Aye. She did. She knew exactly what she was asking.

He shook his head. And there it was, his revenge meant more than her. For some reason, he believed her father had killed his. It couldn't be true, but anger was a bitter, consuming thing.

No matter how honorable men thought it to be, retribution destroyed everything good.

He wanted a justice that would soothe his soul, but it wouldn't change the past. It wasn't because she didn't care for him; it was because she cared too much that she said, "I never want to see you again."

Two men came up between her and Giric. The earl's guards.

Then the grip on her arm loosened as Lord Roger turned to her and latched onto her chin. He squeezed so hard that she winced and gasped as his nails dug into her cheeks. "No one lies to me." He glowered and tilted nearer to hiss into her ear. "You told me you'd not given yourself to anyone."

"Let her go," Giric called, sounding closer. She glanced over to see the earl's men blocked his progression and had swords drawn toward him.

"You may have command over her brother currently, but she is mine." Lord Roger's controlled fury belted back at Giric.

"Take her back and guard her in my room until I arrive." Only one man had dared lay a hand on her before without her permission—her uncle, the day her father had come for her. And if she'd not fought back later that day, her older brother would still be alive.

She couldn't rebel against Lord Roger until she knew Eddie was safe.

She let Lord Roger's men cart her away because he was the only man that could free her brother, even if her father wouldn't spend his last days at peace with family. Eddie had his whole life ahead of him.

A shiver ran down her spine. Lord Roger was cold and aloof, but this was the first time she was actually afraid of him.

~

Giric's fists clenched at his sides. In all the years of anger he'd held onto about his father's demise, he'd never felt a rage so hot as when he'd seen the Earl of Bruton squeeze Jennet's chin and hiss at her. He hadn't heard what the man had said, but he'd seen the fear in her eyes. He'd stepped forward to defend her, but the earl's men had pulled their swords and stood between them.

As the men drew Jennet away, the earl turned to him, a smug look on his face. "I'll still honor our deal, but Lady Jennet is mine."

Giric started toward him. "She doesn't want you. Have yer men release her."

"Touch me, and you'll never see Baron Gillingham," the snake calmly replied.

Giric stopped, every muscle in his body tense and out of sync. How had this happened?

"I'll send the documents immediately. But you are to stay away from Lady Jennet," the earl ordered, then pivoted and strutted away.

He wanted to follow the pompous arse, but there was nothing he could do, and he still had Edward to contend with. If he left the man unattended, he could just rise up and walk off. Then Giric would have nothing.

So, he watched the earl stride back to the castle to fulfill his earlier demands.

No, no, no… This was not how his day was to end. He and Jennet were to be walking down the chapel's aisle to meet a priest, and his enemy was supposed to be delivered to his door. Now another man was claiming rights to the woman he loved. His revenge was on its way, but it felt hollow.

Jennet had spoken of her family as he had his clan. She loved them, and he'd set his sights on destroying them.

He turned to his captive, who still sat quietly on the ground. Giric paced, fisting and unfisting his hands, trying to make sense of everything that had just happened and fighting the urge to leave his prisoner and his revenge to run after Jennet. The ache beneath his breastbone was similar to the loss on the day of his father's death.

He let his memory go back to that day. Anything to help him stay on course and bring back the pain because now he doubted everything.

"Did you know that our father has not been right since that trip to Scotland?" Edward's voice held sadness.

"Did the guilt over killing three innocent people devour him?" He tried to inject anger into the words as he searched for the bitterness he'd felt over the years. A void deeper than that chasm had invaded his chest as he fought to take a simple breath without new pain enveloping him.

"In a way, but it's not what you think."

Giric looked away. Did he want to know what really happened that day?

A merchant from the camp passed by selling spirits. He purchased a full flask and sat next to Edward. He took a large swig. It burned, but he welcomed the heat, then he handed it to Jennet's brother.

"The fire wasn't Jennet's fault, but she always blamed herself."

Giric's hands shook. Jennet had been there. Nae, that was not possible. She would have been a child.

"Start from the beginning." Giric grabbed the stout drink and took another long gulp.

"Our uncle hated our father." Edward took the flask for a swallow and handed it back to Giric.

"Go on." He nodded because he'd gotten that from Jennet before.

"He absconded with Jennet, took her to Scotland, and pretended she was his child for five years. When my father finally tracked them down, there was a fight. She was so young. She didn't know better."

"What happened?" His nails dug into his palms as a picture started to form in his mind.

"Our uncle had Father pinned to the ground, beating him. She tried to stop the fight by picking up the first thing she could and throwing it at our uncle." Edward reached for the flask again. Giric handed it to him and watched as the man took a large swig. "It was a lamp."

He shook his head as pieces of Jennet's tale replayed in his head and mingled with Edward's words.

"The rushes caught immediately. A man ran in and pulled Jennet from the building, then he went back in for Father. The stranger was able to bring him out, but Father had burns all over his body."

"No one knew that our brother Richard had also come in to try to save them. Except maybe the stranger because after he saved Father, he ran back into the building a third time. No one else came out, and when the flames had consumed everything and no one else appeared, Jennet took our father to a healer."

Gooseflesh spread across his limbs. "Jennet was the little girl with the bow."

"Aye. That would have been her. She's always had an affinity for the weapon. Our mother taught her."

He didn't know what to say.

Edward continued. "The stranger must have been your father. But we never knew who saved her and Father."

"She was so young. 'Twasn't her fault." Giric pictured the girl with the page's haircut.

"It's why she's worked so hard to take care of all of us. She blamed herself for all of it."

Giric took the drink back and inhaled two large gulps. "I thought 'twas the girl with the bow who died in the fire, but 'twas yer brother. No' her. That's why her stance was so familiar."

It had all been a mistake. One caused by an angry man's vengeance, and now Jennet was doomed to a life she didn't want because of his need for recompense. His heart ached. He'd just taken her choice away from her again.

No one had murdered his father. He'd died attempting to save a boy from a fire.

He had died an honorable death.

There wasn't enough malted spirits whisky in all of England to wash away the guilt that clung to him like the mist on the moors back home. Jennet was innocent, and it was time she stopped having to pay for bitter men's grievances.

"I change my demand." Jennet would probably never forgive him, but he could still do the right thing.

"Ah, and what will you do, Sir Giric?" Edward reached for the flask.

"For yer freedom, Jennet will have her own. She will have the right to make her own decisions."

"I agree, but that puts me in a bind. How do I handle Lord Roger, who challenged me for her hand?"

"We will put it in writing. This has been public. Does anyone else know of your previous wager?"

"No."

"Then ours will overrule it. And if he protests, I will seek him out. That man will never put his hands on her again." Rage reigned over the heartache as he thought of the earl.

Giric stood and held out a hand for Edward. "Shall we head to the castle and draw up the agreement?"

"Aye."

A little while later, as they signed the papers, Edward turned to him. "Would you like to come with me to give them the news?"

"Nae. I dinnae think she will wish to see me now. 'Tis enough to know she will be able to chart her own course." Even as he said the words, the pain invaded again. Would she be able to forgive him for what he had done?

"And what if she still chooses you?" Edward looked as if he believed there might still be a chance for them. But Giric couldn't let that hope in—it would crush him anew if he did, and she didn't forgive him.

"Then she will know where to find me," he said as he walked away.

CHAPTER 17

*I*t felt as if hours had passed since Eddie burst into Roger's room accompanied by some of Lord Yves's men to demand the earl release her. Giric had changed his mind about the conditions of her brother's release.

He truly hadn't known who she was, and even more meaningful was that Eddie pulled her aside and told her how much he liked and respected Sir Giric.

"He did this for you." Eddie smiled.

Once he'd finished, she told Eddie of her conversation with Sybil. Roger had been pushing her into marrying Eddie. Roger's estate had mounted serious debts, and another earl had started putting pressure on him. He'd thought an alliance with Eddie would help, and when Sybil hadn't been able to secure Jennet's brother's interest, he'd threatened to give her in marriage to a newly widowed neighboring baron who was known to beat his wife. None of it made Sybil any less guilty, but now they knew it was more than just her obsession with Eddie that led to her actions.

When Eddie proposed to Ada, Roger had set his sights on Jennet and her dowry, hoping to secure both in one fell swoop. He didn't really want her—it had been all about his debts.

After the confrontation, they'd gone back to her chamber to let Ada know they were safe and tell her the news of what had transpired.

It was already dark when Jennet found herself running through the halls to find Giric. He wasn't in his room. Her heart sank as she wondered if he'd left for Scotland already. She skipped down the stairs, and there was no sight of him in the great hall. Then she remembered their special spot. The gardens.

The pressure on her heart eased when she saw him sitting on their bench. His thumbs ran over the material of the kerchief she'd given him. The bells tolled for the curfew, and his head dipped. Did he truly think her affection was that fragile, that she wouldn't forgive him for what he had done? But she hadn't said the words held so closely in her heart. He didn't know how she truly felt.

Giric drew the cloth to his nose and breathed in.

She stepped out of the shadows. "You must have won a lady's heart to collect such a favor."

His head snapped up to meet her regard. She saw hope in his eyes, and he seemed to be holding his breath.

"I am afraid that my lady will not forgive my lapse in honor."

"And do you think she should?"

"I believe the lady has had enough of others making decisions for her and she should choose. I am afraid I am at her mercy."

"And what might you do to regain a lady's trust?" She eased onto the bench, so close their legs were touching.

He opened his mouth to speak, but she covered his lips with her finger. His warm breath moved around her as his chest rose and fell.

"What if what she wants in return is too much for a knight to offer?"

"The lady is worth any price." His fingers closed around hers, and he gently curled her hand in his, placing a sweet kiss on top of the sensitive flesh.

Her insides clenched and heated with the need to have him nearer. "And what if she demands your undying loyalty, your devotion, and…your love."

"She may not ken it, but she has had those things since the first moment her hand touched mine." He swiveled his palm so that it was flush with hers as it had been the first night they'd danced.

"Then kiss me, knight, and prove that you are worthy of my affections." As she trailed her fingers across his cheek, she could see the bruises he'd earned in battle. Some she now knew he had earned saving Eddie's life.

His hand threaded through her hair and drew her near. But instead of his lips landing on hers, they moved to her ear. His warm breath sent chills down her spine. "Ye will always be the only woman for me. I pledge everything that I am to ye, Jennet. I love ye."

Her breath caught at the raw emotion she heard in his heavy lilt. The one that had wrapped itself around her and taken her senses. His lips landed on hers, and the embrace was magical. It soothed the hurt of the day, spoke of intimate nights ahead, and promised security in the future.

When he finally pulled back, she met his heated gaze straight on. "Then, Sir Giric, your revenge against my family is complete, and you have earned my undying love."

"Then 'tis the sweetest vengeance I shall ever know. I will cherish it for the rest of my life."

EPILOGUE

Isle of Skye, MacDonald lands
August 1194

The sun dipped and almost hid behind a thick wall of tall green pines, casting a warm glow of the long summer dusk over the land he loved. Giric stepped to the edge of the field, taking in his wife's hypnotic routine. The movements imbued him with a sense of peace and contentment he'd thought he'd never know. He could watch her practice for hours.

Apparently, the rest of their clan could as well because she'd gathered an audience of MacDonalds who jested with each other on the side of the clearing, amazed by her accuracy with the bow. They'd long stopped betting whether she could hit the target and now only wagered on whether she could split an arrow or how many she would land dead center.

Jennet let loose an arrow, relaxed and lowered her bow, then turned to him. She smiled, and his heart soared. She had this way of knowing where he was, and he quite liked how attuned they had become to each other. As she turned toward him, he was rewarded with a view of her full, round belly.

Their first babe would be here soon.

He motioned to the onlookers to retrieve her arrows so that his wife didn't have to walk across the field. Then he strode out to where she stood.

"I was thinking." She gave him a small smile but didn't continue.

"Aye. What about, my lady love?"

"Our child." She paused, took a deep breath, then lay her hand on her midsection. "If it's a boy, I wish to call him Richard."

"After yer newly returned king?" He was surprised by the request. It must have shown on his face because she laughed.

"No. After the brother I lost. The one that your father died trying to save."

"I would like that." Giric took her arm and led her toward the cottage his brother had given them upon their return. "For a moment, I was worried that ye might be missing England."

"No, only my brothers and Ada, but they said they'd visit once her babe is a little older."

"Are you happy here, then?"

"Aye, I have never felt freer than I do here with you and among the clan. They have given me a warm welcome and a sense of belonging."

He liked that she now considered herself a member of their extended family. "Still, ye seem solemn. What brought ye out to practice today?"

"Ada sent word. Sybil has been consigned to a convent."

"'Tis a just sentence."

She nodded. "I agree. It's the best possible outcome."

"Is there more news?"

"Aye, Lord Roger has been sent to prison."

"For what?" After traveling to the south to meet Jennet's father, he and Eddie had attempted to pay the man a call to discuss his behavior, but they had been denied admittance to his estate.

"His debtors caught up to him. Lord Roger's cousin has petitioned to take over his lands."

"Good. How is your brother faring?"

Jennet's father had succumbed to his illness shortly after they had arrived. Giric was thankful that his wife had been able to see the man one last time, and that he'd been able to meet him, to hear stories of what he'd been like before the incident that had changed all their lives. He'd also been able to find peace in knowing the truth about what had happened that day.

"Ada says he's doing well, but I knew he would."

A boy ran up to hand Jennet her arrows. "Thank you," she said as she took them and placed them back in the quiver.

The lad skipped away.

Jennet's eyes widened. "The babe is stirring."

She took his hand, and lovingly placed it on her growing stomach. Her smile was genuine, and joy sparked in his chest. She had been nervous about what was to come next due to her mother's death, but they'd found two of the best healers on the island to be present for the birth. Her fears had been dampened, and her worry had turned to excitement.

"I have two more requests."

"Aye, my love. Name them."

"If the babe is a girl, I wish to call her Saorsa. The name means freedom."

"I like it. 'Tis perfect."

She faced him straight on. "And I want our children to have the same choices my brothers and I were given. They

147

147

should be allowed to marry for affection and not out of obligation."

"I agree. I'm thankful every day that yer parents made that pact." He placed a small kiss on her temple.

"I as well, for if they hadn't, I would not have you."

"Now, may I ask a favor?"

"Aye, Giric."

"Let's go home so that I can show ye how thankful I am to have ye."

"Aye, husband. I would like that." Her smile reached his soul and bathed him in contentment.

"I love ye, Jennet."

"And I love you."

He took her hand in his, and they strode home.

~

Thank you for reading THE HIGHLAND KNIGHT'S REVENGE! Please consider leaving a review. I read them all. I love hearing from readers and reviews help me when I'm plotting my next book.

~

She desired only one kiss, but what she received was so much more!
The next book in the Midsummer Knights series Laurel O'Donnell's MY VICTORIOUS KNIGHT

Check out all the books in the Midsummer Knights series:
Forbidden Warrior by Kris Kennedy
The Highlander's Lady Knight by Madeline Martin
The Highlander's Dare by Eliza Knight
The Highland Knight's Revenge by Lori Ann Bailey
My Victorious Knight by Laurel O'Donnell

An Outlaw's Honor by Terri Brisbin
Never if Not Now by Madeline Hunter

Sign up for my newsletter to see a behind the scenes look at my writing life, get exclusive content, and stay up to date on my latest releases.
LoriAnnBailey.com

ABOUT THE AUTHOR

Lori Ann Bailey is a best-selling author and winner of the National Readers' Choice Award and Holt Medallion for Best First Book and Best Historical, Lori writes hunky highland heroes and strong-willed independent lasses finding their perfect matches in the Highlands of historic Scotland.

She's lived in Mississippi, Ohio, Manhattan, Pennsylvania, and London, but chose to settle in Vienna, VA with her husband and four children. When not writing or reading, Lori enjoys time with her real-life hero and kids or spending time walking or drinking wine with her friends.

Find out more about Lori at her website:

http://loriannbailey.com/

Made in the USA
Middletown, DE
12 January 2021